A DUKE FOR DAISY

THE BLOOMING BRIDES BOOK 1

ELLIE ST. CLAIR

CONTENTS

Chapter 1 1
Chapter 2 6
Chapter 3 12
Chapter 4 20
Chapter 5 28
Chapter 6 36
Chapter 7 45
Chapter 8 54
Chapter 9 61
Chapter 10 67
Chapter 11 75
Chapter 12 83
Chapter 13 89
Chapter 14 97
Chapter 15 103
Chapter 16 112
Chapter 17 119
Chapter 18 128
Epilogue 134
About the Author 139
Also by Ellie St. Clair 141

THE DUKE SHE WISHED FOR

Chapter 1 145

Facebook: Ellie St. Clair

Cover by AJF Designs

Do you love historical romance? Receive access to a free ebook, as well as exclusive content such as giveaways, contests, freebies and advance notice of pre-orders through my mailing list!

Sign up here!

Also By Ellie St. Clair

Standalone
Unmasking a Duke
Christmastide with His Countess

Happily Ever After
The Duke She Wished For
Someday Her Duke Will Come
Once Upon a Duke's Dream
He's a Duke, But I Love Him
Loved by the Viscount
Because the Earl Loved Me

Searching Hearts
Duke of Christmas
Quest of Honor
Clue of Affection
Hearts of Trust
Hope of Romance

Promise of Redemption

The Unconventional Ladies
Lady of Mystery
Lady of Fortune

Blooming Brides
A Duke for Daisy

1

1813

"Oh, but Daisy, you must!"

"Who says I must?"

"Mother, Father, you say so, do you not?"

Their father sighed as he broke a roll of bread in half, slowly buttering it as though the process of eating would prevent the necessity of responding to their bickering. But, of course, it only stalled it.

"By all means we would like to see Daisy marry," he said, then stuffed the bread inside his heavily jowled cheeks.

Iris grinned triumphantly, but Daisy chose to ignore her.

"However," he continued between mouthfuls. "We certainly will not force her to do so. If Daisy chooses to remain home, working at the inn, then so be it."

Iris bristled, shaking her deep chestnut curls behind her back.

"You are saying that only because you need Daisy's help with the inn," she pouted, and Daisy looked up at her, hoping Iris could read the warning in her eyes. The last thing they needed right now was for their mother to go into one of her fits. Iris pursed her lips but understood Daisy's unspoken admonishment.

"I am jesting, Mother, Father, surely you must know that?" she asked, her practiced smile curling on her red lips, those that made most men stumble at her feet. Their father didn't seem to overly care about her words — he didn't about most things, they found — but it was too late to stop their mother's hysterics.

"Oh, Iris, surely you cannot mean such a thing?" their mother asked, her voice rising with every word. Wisps of her hair, once brown but now graying, escaped the cap on her head. "Surely you know that your father and I want nothing more than for Daisy to be happy? When Lord Mansel shoved her off, you know how distraught we were!"

Alice Tavner certainly had been distraught when the local baron's son had tossed her eldest daughter over for another. As for Daisy? It wasn't as though her heart had been broken, but the dismissal had left anger simmering within her, that she could be so callously abandoned without much thought whatsoever. She had assumed Stephen was courting her because he was interested in marrying her, but no, she had just turned out to be a village woman with whom to pass the time as he waited for the woman he would truly marry.

From the seat next to her, Marigold spoke up. "Daisy never much liked him anyway."

Daisy could almost roll her eyes. Were her sisters purposely attempting to send their mother into apoplexy?

"Not like him?" Alice repeated, breathing heavily. "Not like *him*? Every unmarried woman within the vicinity liked him! Daisy was fortunate enough to capture his attention for a moment or two, but then that hussy came into town and with a few blinks of her eyelashes, it was as though Daisy never existed!"

"While I thank you all for reliving this experience," Daisy said dryly, "could we move on to another topic of conversation?"

"I think this is important," Iris said stubbornly. "For you must find someone else, Daisy, or how are the rest of us supposed to marry? I have to wait for you *and* for Marigold to wed before I will have the opportunity, and I have been more than ready for some time."

"While I question your readiness, you are speaking nonsense," Daisy said practically. "There is no rule that says you must wait for your elder sisters to marry. I'm sure Mother and Father would be fine if you found someone for yourself, is that not so?"

She looked to her parents, who didn't answer her question directly, though her mother let out a theatrical sigh, as though all had been lost for her daughters after Lord Mansel had forgotten Daisy.

"You see?" Daisy said with a smile, lifting a hand. "What I think is truly holding you back, Iris, is that you have far too *many* men who are interested in you, and you in them."

"That is not true!" her sister exclaimed, her deep blue eyes widening.

Daisy wished her own looked something like her sister's. In fact, she often wished she looked much more like her sister in all ways. While she considered all three of her younger siblings to be beautiful, Iris stood out, perhaps, in part, due to her vivaciousness. Daisy's own eyes were a blue-green that were hardly ever noticed, and she was too tall, too broad, too strong. It helped when it came to tasks around their parents' inn, but certainly not when it came to catching the attention of a man.

Stephen Carter, at the time the son of Lord Mansel, had noticed her one day only because he had nearly accidentally trampled her with his horse. After his apology, they had shared a laugh and a polite conversation. She had been shocked when he had continued her acquaintance at a dance at his father's house, furthering it by calling upon her more and more frequently, most often to go walking. But the moment of his father's passing, when he had become Baron himself, it was as though nothing between them had ever existed. Instead, he was suddenly impossibly interested in Lady Almira Darlington, apparently a close family friend, who had come to visit following the mourning period.

Daisy could admit to herself now that her interest in Stephen had been starting to wear thin, but she hadn't felt it was appropriate to say anything while he was in mourning, his father having so recently passed. Apparently, the dissolution of their relationship hadn't bothered him in the least.

"What does it matter what I think?" Daisy asked with a sigh. "If I ever marry, I'm sure I will be the last of us to do so. Besides, now that I have thought further about it, it only makes sense that I find a man who would be interested in taking this inn over himself. We have no brothers, so who else will help Mother and Father?"

Her words somewhat calmed her mother, who now looked more contemplative. Yes, Daisy had chosen the correct tactic to maintain the peace. Thank goodness. Her youngest sister, Violet, looked to her with a grateful smile. The girl hated conflict more than any of them. If it ever escalated too quickly, she would run to her room and hide.

Her sisters — Violet, as well as Marigold — were the one reason Daisy typically chose not to allow Iris to cause too much discord with the entire family about. Daisy would wait until they were alone to tell Iris exactly what she thought.

"Oh, that reminds me," their father said, lifting a finger from his place at the head of the table. "We have a new boarder. He will be arriving this week."

"How long a stay will he be here for?" Daisy asked as she began to think of which room he should be lodged in and what they would need to have prepared for him. "And when exactly does he arrive?"

Her father looked thoughtful for a moment, as though he had completely forgotten. Daisy sighed inwardly. She did wish he would write these things down. "Perhaps in a week, perhaps two. I cannot say I completely remember."

Daisy attempted to smile and set aside her concerns at her father's memory, as well as the extra work it would create for her, being unaware of this man's arrival date. They would simply have to be ready, that was all.

The Wild Rose Inn would not suffer any loss to its reputation, of that Daisy would make sure.

2

Major-General Nathaniel Huntingwell began his slow hobble toward the makeshift office down what seemed to be a never-ending corridor.

Finally, his leg had healed enough for him to rise from his bed with the assistance of a cane. It was time to return to the action, to defeat Bonaparte and his annoyingly stubborn armies.

Nathaniel was aware that with the risk he had taken, he was lucky to be alive. But that was no matter. The reward had been far greater than any had ever imagined.

While Nathaniel's fight had ended with a bayonet slicing halfway through his calf and a head injury, the origin of which he was entirely unaware, his army had won the battle, and that was all that had mattered to him.

Nathaniel had awoken in a temporary field hospital not far from the battle site. His head should hopefully be fine, he was told, but his leg would likely never be the same again.

Never the matter. He might not be able to ever run again, but he could ride, he could plan, he could lead. He was more fortunate than most in that they hadn't immediately amputated the leg, and it had healed well enough for him to put some weight on it. It was time to return to the strategy table, and he welcomed the news that the general had arrived — likely to send him back into battle, he thought, the need to return to the front nearly overwhelming him when he finally made it to the door at the end of the hall.

He lifted his hand to knock but was startled when a voice from inside spoke first.

"Come in."

Nathaniel turned the knob and pushed the door open, the surprise clearly evident on his face.

"I could hear you coming for the last five minutes," General Collins said, a slight smile on the face that was about twenty years Nathaniel's senior. "You certainly wouldn't find yourself surprising any enemy with that leg of yours."

"Perhaps not," Nathaniel responded, though he bristled at Collins' words. "Give me a week and you will hear nothing."

"I would be impressed if it were so," the general said, then went straight to the reason for his visit. "I have heard that you have been recovering very well. However, I have also been told by the doctors that you will never have full use of your leg again and will require a cane for the rest of your life."

Nathaniel's urge to defend himself surged within him, and had he been speaking to anyone but another officer who outranked him, he certainly would have done so.

"I beg to disagree," he said instead, and the general simply sighed, frowning beneath his large mustache.

"I commend you for your fight, Major-General Huntingwell," he said, "However you have other orders now."

Nathaniel nodded, eager to hear them, wondering where he would next be sent.

"It beings with some news," the general began, reading from a piece of paper beside him. "Your uncle, the Duke of Greenwich, has died."

"Oh," Nathaniel sat back, taking in the general's revelation. His uncle had always been a commanding figure, the type of man one thought would live forever. "How?"

"It was an illness," the general explained. "The doctors are not entirely sure what it was, but apparently it included high fever and swept rapidly through the village of his country home. Many survived, many did not."

He paused.

"His son was also so unfortunate."

"Charles?" Grief filled him now at the thought of two of his relatives gone, in a matter of moments — at least, that was how it felt to him. "Surely, no others in the family?"

His aunt had passed some time ago now, but Charles had sisters, and he pictured their sweet, innocent faces.

"The girls remain well," the general said. "I believe they managed to pull through."

Nathaniel nodded grimly. Charles had been married but last year, and he knew there were hopes for children. He wondered if any had been born. Charles' poor wife.

"However, as Charles and his wife were yet to bear any children—" That answered his question, "—you are aware of what that means?"

Nathaniel attempted to control the emotions roiling within him. What was the general going on about? What did this have to do with him? But— of course. Goodness.

"I am now the Duke," he said, his voice raw, filled with both grief and shock. His entire life was changing in a matter of moments. Could the general not have prepared him a bit better?

But no. The man had much more to be concerned about than Nathaniel's emotions. Of which, he should attempt to get under control himself.

"You are the new Duke of Greenwich," the general confirmed with a nod. "Congratulations."

Nathaniel ran a hand over his face as he attempted to process all of the information.

"What do you mean by my new orders?"

"You will assume the role of duke in due fashion," the general said. "But it will be some time before you do."

"Because…" Nathaniel began warily, unsure if he wanted to hear any more.

"Because of the important documents you were able to recover from Bonaparte's belongings during your last battle. Your bravery in infiltrating the enemy's camp did not go unnoticed. The documents — his plans — were found upon your person once you were taken to the hospital."

Nathaniel nodded. It had been one of the key components of the battle, for him to achieve the impossible and gain access to the plans. It had been an intricate strategy, one in which he had to assume the identity of a French soldier. The fact that he spoke the language fluently had helped him to earn the role, as did his nature to take whatever risk was necessary in order to protect his country.

"However, our sources tell us that the French army is aware of your theft. They also know that you went down in battle, though fortunately you were recovered by our own soldiers before the French realized who you were and what you had on your person. What they don't know is your fate. They hope that you are buried in a mass grave, the documents along with you. We do not want them to know that we retrieved them. As you are aware, they have as many spies within England as we do within France. Therefore, you will return to England for a time, and hide until, at least, we can use the information you accessed and surprise Boney and his men where they next plan to attack."

"Hide?" Nathaniel said, hearing his voice rise but unable to stop it. "How can I hide? I must be part of this attack. For God's sake, man, if it wasn't for me, you would have no idea where to even begin! I should be alongside you, helping to strategize and then follow through. I have been waiting for this — it is the reason I have recovered so quickly, in order to return to the battlefield."

"I understand that," the general said, his voice calm, though the years were showing in the concerned creases of his forehead as Nathaniel spoke. "Unfortunately, it is not to be, at least not at the moment."

"But—"

"I have a friend," the general continued, as though Nathaniel hadn't said anything at all. "I served with him years ago, when we first began fighting the French. He is married now, has a family — four daughters, if you can believe that. He and his wife run an inn in Southwold. The man has gambled away much of his money and needs some additional income. Which is fortunate for us, as he has agreed to take in soldiers who need a quiet place to stay for a time."

Nathaniel ran through all of this in his mind as he sat back in the chair, a hand upon his head.

"So I am to go and hide — doing nothing — in a seaside village while you attack Napoleon in the location I helped determine?"

"Yes, I suppose that is the way of it."

Despair filled Nathaniel at the thought of such inaction.

"I don't know if I have it within me."

"Those are your orders, Major-General. I expect you to follow them. Now. *Your grace.*"

Nathaniel started at the formal address, as he had forgotten for a moment the general's initial news.

"Thank you for your service to your country. And do enjoy your stay at the Wild Rose Inn."

3

Daisy lifted an apple, inspecting it on all sides before nodding and placing it in her bag. She paid the vendor and continued to walk along the tables of the marketplace, selecting food for the family and their guests after carefully studying the quality and the pricing. Their father had been quite clear that the money needed to be stretched tightly over the next few months, though why, Daisy had no idea. Of course, when questioned about it, he had no response beyond a grunt so they dropped it, though Daisy would have liked to have known more.

If only she had been his son and not his daughter, she thought with a sigh. Then, perhaps, he would treat her with more respect.

"Daisy!"

She turned to see her friend, Millie, running toward her, her blonde curls already falling out of her bonnet.

"Millie," Daisy exclaimed, reaching out a hand toward her. "How are you?"

"Very well," Millie said with a smile as she swung what

seemed to be an empty basket on her arm. "I'm running late, as usual, but I must hurry to find enough to prepare dinner for Father tonight. He's been quite busy."

Daisy nodded. Millie's father was the town's blacksmith. It was only the two of them within their family, which left Millie to look after the household and help with the shop. Perhaps that was what had always drawn Daisy and Millie together — their need to take responsibility.

"It looks like you've been busy."

"Yes, well, in addition to the Johnsons, we have a new boarder arriving soon. Father told us last week to expect him 'soon,' though he was rather loose on any details, so it's best to be prepared."

Millie laughed at that, though she sobered somewhat at the initial news. "How long do you think the Johnsons will stay?"

"I'm not sure," Daisy said with a shrug. "Their house and barn burned a couple of months ago now, though the new buildings should be near finished, what with all the help they've received. I know we've been allowing them to stay for next to nothing, however, so it would be good for both them to have a new home to return to as well as for us to be able to rent the rooms to higher paying customers."

"In due time," said Millie, placing a hand on Daisy's arm in support. "I'm off for a quick stop to pick up some fish. I shall see you soon, Daisy — farewell!"

Daisy smiled as she watched Millie continue to where the young man with whom she was smitten was selling his wares. Daisy waved a hand goodbye as she continued on her way to The Wild Rose Inn, which her mother had named, of course.

Ah, her mother and her fascination with all things floral. She loved her mother, truly she did, but she would never fully understand her, that was certain. The two of them were as different as... well, a tulip and an oak tree, she thought with a laugh.

Daisy was still smiling to herself as she used her shoulder to push open the door of the inn, taking the shortest way through the front, for there should be no one about at this hour, the Johnsons at their farm, leaving only her family about.

She turned to enter the foyer, but as she did, she crashed into an immovable object, which was very hard, very strong, and completely unrelenting.

Her two baskets went flying from her hands, and as Daisy fell to the ground on her bottom, for a moment it was as though it was raining fruits, vegetables, loaves of bread, and blocks of cheese all around her.

Daisy was stunned for a moment until she looked up to see just what had caused her to fall.

A man stood staring down at her — a stranger, which wasn't usual in these parts. He looked like a giant from here, though Daisy wasn't sure if that was only because of her current vantage point. He might have been handsome, his sandy brown hair worn too long, curling about his ears, his nose slender but slightly crooked, as though it had been broken. But what caught her the most was the solemn expression he wore, one that looked down upon her as though he was far her better.

As she studied him, she waited for him to apologize and to hold out a hand to help her to her feet. But he did nothing except stand there.

She surged up as she began to try to salvage the food that was littered around her, looking up at him time and again as she scooped up the food.

"Do you speak English?" she finally burst out, and he nodded, narrowing his eyes at her.

"Of course."

"Ah, so you are *choosing* to say nothing," she said, angry now at what should have been a simple apology on his part. "Did you not see me as I came through the door? Could you not have taken a step back? Or, perhaps, apologized?"

He leaned back against the door now, crossing his arms.

"I believe we ran into one another. You were at fault as much as I was."

"Pardon me?" she exclaimed. "My arms were full! And on that note, perhaps you could help me here?"

"I apologize, but I cannot."

"You cannot or you will not?" she huffed, though she gave him no time to respond. "I am not sure who you are, but you are *certainly* no gentleman."

"That is much to surmise when we have hardly met."

"I know enough," she said as she finished gathering the food, much of which was now bruised and dirty. She would do her best to wash it off, but she had a feeling her father would somehow blame her for this. Not directly, no, but in his sigh, in his tone, and in the look in his eyes, she would know his disappointment.

"Did you find what you were looking for inside?"

"I did not," he said dryly. "It seems The Wild Rose Inn is currently unoccupied."

"It is not," she retorted. "My mother and sister should be about."

"Ah, so you are one of the daughters," he said, recognition coming into his eyes.

"I am," she said with a nod. "And just who would you be?"

"Ah, you've met!"

Daisy turned toward her father's voice through the open door as he strode up the walk behind her. Much to her surprise, he greeted the man in front of her with a warm and hearty handshake. This was strange.

"Unfortunately, we have not yet had the pleasure of an introduction," she said, and her father's attention finally turned back toward her.

"Well then, this is my daughter Daisy," her father said, waving an arm in her direction, though he kept his attention on the newcomer. "Daisy, this gentleman is Mr. Nathanial Hawke, our new boarder."

NATHANIEL MIGHT ONLY NEWLY BE a duke himself, but he had been the grandson of a duke, the member of a noble family, for his entire life. Never before had a woman so far below his own standing treated him with such arrogance, such impropriety. Though she did not know him to be a duke — a fact which must certainly remain in secrecy, following the general's warnings, hence his assumed surname — he was a guest in her home, and he expected to be treated as such.

Upon learning his identity, she simply nodded and brushed by him, continuing on her way.

In truth, he actually would have lent a hand toward her, both in helping her off the ground and collecting the food, but if he bent down upon his leg, he didn't think he could get back up. Perhaps if he had his cane he could have, but he was quite determined to get along without it, if for no other reason than to prove everyone wrong about his condition.

He followed Elias Tavner into the inn. He had a hard time picturing him as a contemporary of the general, but then, Tavner had clearly settled into his role as a family man and innkeeper, whereas the general would forever be part of the fight.

Nathaniel had actually just arrived at the inn when the daughter had pushed open the door and caught him in the back. He had turned in time to see her go flying backward, the food falling about her disastrously, her face clearly displaying the fact that she blamed him for her current position.

He had been about to apologize, but he wasn't quite sure how to explain that he couldn't help her due to his injury. He didn't want to use that as an excuse and yet... Then she had begun to speak, and he could hardly get a word in, nor did he know what to say in response to her anger as he felt his defenses go up.

So he had simply ignored her. It seemed the easier thing to do.

Nathaniel slowly followed Tavner through the inn. The foyer was small, leading into a larger sitting room area for the guests. It was true to the name of the inn, both the walls and the furniture patterned in all manner of floral designs, though not necessarily roses. A door on one side led to what Tavner told him was the kitchen, while he informed him that a back door was the entrance to the family quarters.

It wasn't a lot of space to entertain oneself in, Nathaniel thought as his family's London home and country estate came to mind.

"Now, as for your bedroom... I'm not entirely sure, actually, which will be yours," Tavner said, looking somewhat embarrassed. "Let me find Daisy."

Daisy? Not this girl again. Did no one else in this house do anything? Soon she appeared, a line creased between her dark brows as he studied him.

"This way," was all she said, curtly, and Nathaniel held

himself back from retorting anything toward her. He looked down at his lone travel bag, then back up at Tavner.

"Do you not have a man for the bags?"

Daisy slowly turned to look at him, incredulity written on her face.

"Are you unable to lift that small bag yourself, Mr. Hawke?"

"Actually," he said, no longer concerned about the excuse of his leg, for he would far prefer enjoying the fact that he could prove her wrong, in order to take the haughty look off her face. "I cannot."

He began to limp forward to follow her, and her eyes widened as she realized that he was injured.

"What happened to you?" she asked forwardly, and he shrugged and responded with a simple, "battle wound."

He thought perhaps the fact he was a soldier might impress her, as it did most other women, but she didn't seem to overly care as she doubled back, hefted his bag into his arms, and then strode down the hall. He certainly hadn't meant for her to carry his things, but he wasn't sure what he could say now.

"Can you climb a set of stairs?" she asked over her shoulder, and Nathaniel looked around for her father, but the man seemed to have disappeared.

"I can."

"Good. Otherwise, you would have to sleep on the chesterfield."

While her point was valid, somehow her tone made it sound like a threat of some sort, which Nathaniel wasn't completely thrilled about, though he began to slowly climb the stairs after her, testing the rail to ensure it would hold his body weight. It was only in moments such as these that the thought crept in that perhaps he was being slightly too stubborn, too proud to forgo the cane, but then he saw himself with it in his hand and he renounced it once again.

She waited for him at the top of the stairs, still holding his bag, which made him feel slightly as less of a man that a woman had to carry his belongings for him. Why didn't this blasted inn have a man to carry it instead? Did that mean most guests carried their own belongings?

Of course, he'd had to do much for himself while in the army, but even there he was treated with deference for his position.

Finally, they stood at the doorway of a room, and she practically threw the bag inside before turning to face him, jumping when she found that he was but inches behind her. He smiled. Good. At least he could manage to disconcert her in one way.

"There you are. I hope it is to your liking."

She stepped back, away from the door and behind him, which allowed him to take a better look into the room, finding that the most he could say for it was that it looked clean. The lone bed was covered in a blanket and a couple of pillows, all which looked rather worn. A carpet lay beneath it, while a small washstand and privacy screen stood in the other corner of the small room, taking up whatever space remained.

Nathaniel began to ask if they might have anything more spacious, but when he turned back around to question her, she was gone.

4

"Who is this man, the new boarder?" Daisy asked her father that night as she and her sisters set the family's supper down upon the table.

"He is recently returned from battle," he responded. "He is staying here on the request of an old friend of mine."

"Why here?" she demanded. "Why can he not go home?"

"He has... extenuating circumstances," her father said. "That is all that I know."

"Very mysterious," Iris said, her eyes shining. "I finally saw him tonight at dinner. He is quite handsome."

"And very conceited," Daisy added, with a stern look to her sister when she rolled her eyes at her in response. "He seems to think we are his servants. When we served food to him and the Johnsons this evening, he kept waiting, as though we were to pour his wine, cut his food, and what, feed it to him on a fork?"

"Perhaps he is from a family where they had servants to

do all of that for him," Marigold said, and Daisy shook her head gently at her tender-hearted sister.

"Even so, he is staying at an inn," she said. "What does he expect?"

Besides the six of them, they had but one maid, who worked where she was needed — most often in the scullery, or at times helping with the cleaning of a chamber upon the departure of a guest. They used to have more staff, a footman as well as a cook, but Daisy's father determined that with four adult women living in his home, they could each do their part and take on some of the responsibility of keeping the inn. Another villager looked after the stables next door, to where any visitors with horses would pay a separate fee.

They all looked up, surprised when they heard a knock on the door of the family quarters, and Violet rose to answer it. She had to look down, for standing there was little Davy Johnson, one of the children of the family currently staying at the inn.

"Hi there, Miss Violet," he said, smiling to show the gap where he had currently lost one of his teeth. "I was sent by Mr. Hawke. He asked where the bell pull was."

"We have no bell pulls," responded Daisy's sister matter-of-factly, and the boy nodded. "That's what I told him. So he told me to come find someone, as he is wanting a bath."

"Oh, for the love of—"

Daisy's father quelled her outburst with a warning glance.

"Davy, please tell Mr. Hawke that we will fill his bath momentarily," he said. "Now, which of you ladies is closest to finishing your dinner?"

Daisy attempted to cover her plate as Davy nodded and left. Typically Daisy was assigned to such matters, but she had no wish to see the man again this evening. She might have a hard time holding her tongue around him.

"Daisy, you and Marigold will go. Have Maria begin to boil the water and she can help you carry it once finished."

"But—"

"No arguments, please."

Daisy sighed and went to find their maid, Maria, whose eyes widened at the request — especially at this time of night! — but she began the work anyway. After returning to the table and quickly finishing her own meal, Daisy rose to begin hauling the water, with Marigold in her wake.

"He certainly seems interesting," Marigold said as they climbed the stairs, her voice only slightly above a whisper. "What do you suppose happened to his leg?"

"I was told a battle wound," Daisy said dryly. "Which could mean anything, I suppose."

"Where did he fight?"

"I have no idea," responded Daisy. "Though I assume if we ask, we will be met only by a haughty stare with which we are apparently supposed to be impressed."

"Do you really think he's that bad?" Marigold asked hesitantly, her blue eyes wide.

Daisy looked down at her sister, who was of average height, though she was lean, which made her look taller than she was.

"I'm not sure," she said with a sigh. "But so far upon my dealings with him, he has been quite demanding and does not seem to have any wish to treat us as anything but servants, which we, most decidedly, are not."

"Though he is a guest in our inn," Marigold pointed out, and Daisy stopped responding. Marigold was right — he was a guest — but even guests should have more manners than this man, should they not? Why did no one else realize that he was a nuisance? She was sure they would, in time, for she doubted he would become any easier to deal with.

When they knocked on his chamber door, they heard no response, and they eased the door open to find the room empty. The two of them found the bathtub, heaved it into the room with much unladylike grunting, and then returned to the kitchens to begin to carry the water for his bath.

The man certainly had excellent timing, for they had just completed filling the copper tub when he appeared in the entry of the room.

"There you are," Daisy said. "I was wondering if perhaps I might have to enjoy this bath myself."

Marigold gasped at her forwardness, but Mr. Hawke only raised an eyebrow, apparently unaffected by her words.

"Have you a wish to join me then?"

Warmth seeped into her cheeks despite the fact that she was very aware he said such a thing only to goad her, and she refused to give in.

"Of course not," she said, holding her nose in the air to show him just what she thought of his words. "We will leave you be."

"A towel?" he asked curtly, and Daisy nodded.

"I will return with it shortly."

"Very good — please make that two," he said, and the moment she and Marigold were out of the room with the door shut firmly behind them, she turned to her sister. "Do you see what I mean?"

Marigold shrugged, apparently unconcerned.

"One would assume that he needs a towel."

"Two towels, apparently."

Marigold laughed.

"What is it about this man that has you so upset?"

"He's just so... so..."

Marigold laid a hand on Daisy's arm, drawing them to a halt as she peered into her sister's eyes.

"Are you attracted to him?"

"No!" Daisy exclaimed. "Absolutely not."

"It would be understandable if you were," Marigold continued, as though she hadn't heard Daisy, but by then they were back downstairs, and Daisy had opened the cupboard, finding two towels. She didn't purposefully find the oldest, most torn near-rags — they just happened to be those on top.

"Do you want me to come back upstairs with you?" Marigold asked, but Daisy shook her head. The faster she could return to Mr. Hawke's chamber and give him his blasted towels, the sooner he could get in the bathtub, making him less likely to complain about cold water and, hopefully, he would go to bed for the night and they wouldn't have to hear from him until morning.

She climbed the stairs and knocked on the door. She heard his voice from within but wasn't entirely sure what he had said through the thick wood of the door. He knew she was returning — likely he was just summoning her to come in. Heaven forbid he would come and open the door himself.

Daisy was rolling her eyes as she pushed open the door.

"Here you are, your towels—"

She forgot what she was saying, what she was doing. For there in the middle of the room, Mr. Hawke reclined in the bathtub, steam seeping out of it around his head and shoulders. He was so large he hardly fit in the small tub. His arms and legs were draped over the edges, and Daisy had full view of the top of a very broad, strong, bronze chest, which was lightly dusted with a smattering of hair that gleamed golden in the light of the candles.

Daisy knew she should drop the towels on the floor, turn around, shut the door, and leave the room immediately. But she was rooted to the spot, unable to move. She was loathe to admit it, but his body was... magnificent. He reminded her of the sculptures she had seen in one of Violet's books, but with a few cuts and bruises, which only made him seem more human.

Finally, her eyes reached the man's face, and her cheeks began to burn when she saw he was staring right back at her with a raised eyebrow.

"See something you like?" he asked drolly, and Daisy narrowed her eyes at him.

"What do you think you are doing?" she demanded, anger taking over the admiration that had momentarily beholden her.

"I am taking a bath," he said, sweeping an arm out, speaking to her as though she were an idiot.

"Why would you enter into the bath when you knew we were coming back with towels?"

"I assumed you would send a man," he responded with a shrug, his shoulder muscles bulging as he did so.

"As you know," she said through gritted teeth, "this inn is lacking men."

"Your father is a man," he returned. "At any rate, it doesn't bother me to have a woman within. You can set the towels on the chair over there."

Daisy could feel her jaw set at his superior tone. She could set them there, could she? She purposefully averted her eyes and walked by him, placing them on the bed, just out of his reach. He could stand chilled in the air for a moment — it wouldn't do him any harm and would actually probably be a good thing, to teach him some humility if nothing else. Daisy smiled to herself as she turned to go, but when she did, she could see his leg, hanging over the edge of the tub, from the other side.

There was a deep, ugly red scar running along the back of his calf. She couldn't be sure, but it looked as though it had been infected at some point. How in the world did he manage to walk on it? Daisy swallowed hard, sympathy for him seeping in through her annoyance, but she shook her head. He had been injured, yes, and she took no pleasure in that — but it didn't give him any right to act the way he did with such an attitude.

"I really would appreciate them on the chair," he said, his voice slightly softer, as though he realized it might help his case. "I'd prefer not to slip on the floor with this bad leg — the one you have been staring at for so long."

"I'm not—" Daisy began to retort, but then took a deep breath. He was clearly attempting to rile her. She refused to give him the satisfaction.

"Unless, of course, you'd like to stay and help me out of the tub. You could then pass me the towel — or not."

Daisy gasped at his words.

"Excuse me?" she burst out. "I am sorry, sir, but I surely hope you did not say such a thing to me. You may be a paying guest, but that gives you *no right* to insult me so."

Her words didn't move him one bit.

"Are you, or are you not the one remaining in the bedchamber of a man lying naked in a bathtub?"

"I'm only here because you asked me to be here!"

"So all I need to do is ask?"

"Agh!" Daisy burst out, knowing she sounded like an idiot but unable to think of anything else to say, so angry she was. Her body was heated now, with ire, embarrassment, and something else that she couldn't quite describe.

She stalked to the door, placing her hand upon the knob. She was about to leave, but she needed to make one thing clear before she did. She turned around to look at his smug face.

"I may be the daughter of an innkeeper, but that doesn't mean that I do not possess morals of any sort. I am an intelligent woman, Mr. Hawke, and I will not be taken for a fool."

And with that she opened the door, slamming it behind her as she strode down the corridor, the sound of his chuckle remaining in her ears every step of the way.

5

Daisy yawned as she and her sisters set the table for the guests' dinner that night. Typically, they served the boarders first, and then they would head in for their own supper. If it had been a busy day — as they usually were — Daisy's head was often near to her plate as she ate, so tired she was.

Tonight was worse than most days, for she had hardly slept at all the night before.

And there was only one man to blame.

"What's wrong with you today, Daisy?" Iris asked. "You've been acting like Violet, with your head anywhere but the present, which is not at all like you."

Violet looked up at that, glaring at her sister for a moment before returning to placing the cutlery around the table.

"It's not an insult, Violet," Iris said with a wave of her hand. "You have imagination. When your head isn't between the pages of a book, that is."

Violet ignored her as Iris' attention returned to Daisy. "So what is the matter?"

"Nothing at all," Daisy said with a shrug. "I just didn't sleep well last night."

"You always sleep well," Marigold said, her brow furrowing. She would know, as the two of them shared a bedroom. "I didn't notice you awake last night."

"Because *you* were sound asleep, snoring away merrily, I might add," Daisy returned with a raised eyebrow, attempting to lighten the situation.

They laughed at one another but were interrupted by the door opening and their mother poking her head into the dining room.

"Girls!" she exclaimed. "Hurry now, the food has been waiting far too long, and we best serve it while it's hot."

"Or else *someone* will be particularly upset," Daisy muttered and Marigold, the only one within earshot, turned to look at her.

"Is that what kept you up last night?" Marigold asked, her gaze perceptive. "The new boarder?"

"Of course not," Daisy responded indignantly. "Why would he?"

Marigold shrugged. "I'm not sure, but your response to him when we set up his bath last night was most unusual. Did something happen when you returned with the towels?"

Daisy paused mid-step as she followed her sisters through the door. She hadn't told Marigold that she had walked in to find Mr. Hawke in the midst of his bath. Somehow, the thought of sharing such a story embarrassed her — maybe because Daisy knew, looking back on it, that she should have turned around and left the moment she opened the door.

But instead, all she could do was picture him as he lay in the bathtub. She had never seen muscles such as his before.

Not that she had seen many — or any — men naked before, especially with drops of water glistening on their bare bodies. When she thought of his golden skin, she couldn't help but compare it to her own paleness, and somehow that led to the thought of them next to one another — a thought which should have repulsed her, and yet actually made her tremble with an entirely different emotion, the one that had begun when she saw him lying there, the one she desperately wanted to ignore.

What was wrong with her? A man had never made her feel such a way before — not even Stephen Carter, who she had thought she would one day marry.

Why, out of all the men in England, should this arrogant, hostile one make her feel such a way? The only way he could be any worse was if he were another baron or entitled gentleman. Clearly he had wealth if he was used to servants waiting upon him to perform every small task. She could hardly imagine how he would act if he had a title as well.

She noticed Marigold was still waiting for a response, and Daisy forced a smile on her face and shook her head.

"No, nothing happened," she said, allowing the door to swing closed behind her as she took a deep breath, knowing that when she returned to the room, it would be to serve the Johnsons as well the very gentleman she couldn't remove from her mind any more than she could from this inn. "Nothing at all."

NATHANIEL BEGAN the slow processes of walking down the stairs to the dining room. The first night he had dressed for supper as he had at home before realizing that here, at the Wild Rose Inn in Southwold, dressing for dinner meant something else entirely. So today, he kept on his casual trousers and linen shirt, wearing only a waistcoat over top. He gripped the railing tightly once more as he started down the stairs. He kept his weight on his right leg, for the most part, half hopping and suspending the left in midair as he started down. Thankfully, no one had yet witnessed the atrocity of his descent. It certainly wasn't regal — not for Mr. Hawke, and most especially not for the Duke of Greenwich.

He managed a tight smile for the Johnson family as the six of them stared at him with very similar gazes, all red hair and green eyes, from Mr. and Mrs. Johnson down to the four children. He determined the eldest girl to be around fifteen, the youngest a boy of about five — Davy, he remembered, the boy who was just as bored as Nathaniel himself and therefore was always pleased to be as helpful as possible.

And bloody hell, was Nathaniel bored. He had only been here three days and already he could hardly stand it. Tomorrow, he resolved, he would leave this inn and make his way around the town to see what else it had to offer, though he didn't suppose it was much at all.

Today he had already perused all that the bookshelf in the corner of the sitting room had to offer, but he was left disappointed. The books were mostly gothic novels and poetry, though he wasn't sure what else he should expect. One of the women obviously liked to read.

He wondered if it was Daisy. He had asked a few questions to each of the sisters, to Tavners himself, and to the Johnsons, which helped him begin to better understand this family. Tavners had inherited the inn shortly after he had returned from his own stint against the French. He and his wife quickly bore children, but try as they might, a son never came. At one point in time, from the sounds of it, there had been additional staff, but they had sold the stables to another townsperson, and now they relied on their daughters to look after the inn.

Was that fair? Nathaniel wondered. Perhaps it was part of the explanation for why Daisy was so dour all of the time — she worked far too hard.

Just then, the woman who was beginning to occupy far too many of his thoughts walked into the room, delicately balancing seven bowls of soup on a tray upon her arms. She must be strong, he thought with some admiration as one of her sisters began to take the bowls from the tray and, one at a time, place them before the guests. He was the last to be served, and as the bowl was set in front of him, he looked up, accidentally catching Daisy's eyes.

He wished he hadn't. In fact, as fun as it had been to tease her with the bath, he now knew he should never have done so. Nathaniel hadn't been sure it would be she who would return with the towels, but he had an inkling it would be, as she seemed to do everything else. He had thought to fluster her, though why, he had no idea. But instead, when he had caught her staring at him, all of his nerves, the signals that he had thought were lost along with the proper use of his leg, began to tingle once more, and he felt more than saw her glance over what was exposed of his naked body.

He wished she would have turned around and fled, to allow her embarrassment to be made apparent to him at another day, another time. But no, she had stood there and continued to look at him, and he had wanted nothing more than to jump out of the tub and crush that tall, strong body against his, taking from her the strength that he now lacked.

For that was the very worst of it. Despite the fact that he would never actually do such a thing with a woman who, though attractive, would test him at every turn, he physically could not lift himself from the bathtub without a great deal of grunting and finagling to have his limbs in just the proper position so that he could rely on his arms and his good leg to allow himself to balance properly. It was quite the ordeal and not one that he would have anyone — least of all Daisy Tavners — witness.

So he had chosen to lie back and grin lazily at her, enjoying the fact that she seemed to be entranced by him. When he had heard her place the towels on the bed and turn around to go, by the halting of her footsteps he had known that she had stopped and was likely staring at his leg. He was well aware of just how ugly it was, though that didn't much bother him. No, it was his own limitations that really tore at him, made him wish it could be otherwise.

Coming back to the present, he winked at her to further disconcert her, and she broke his stare, the blue-green ocean of her eyes darting around the room to look anywhere but at him. So, she was still embarrassed by yesterday's encounter, was she?

Unfortunately, the thought only made him even more aware of her presence, which annoyed him. Why should he care what the loud, opinionated woman thought? He was a guest of her inn, and she should treat him as such — whether he was naked in the bath or in his dinner attire here at the table.

"Good evening to all of the lovely Tavners women," he said instead to the whole of them. While her sisters smiled at him, Daisy continued to ignore him, so he continued. "Thank you for your fine hospitality."

One of the other girls — Marigold, he thought her name was — began to thank him in a soft tone, though her voice was still loud enough to drown out whatever it was that Daisy was muttering.

"My apologies, Miss Daisy," he said, unsure of how else to differentiate between the sisters, "But did you say something?"

"I did not," came her terse reply, despite the fact he knew better.

"I could have sworn I saw your lips moving."

"Just singing to myself," she said with a bright and clearly forced smile. "I do love to sing."

"You do not!" exclaimed one of the other sisters, who began to provide soup spoons, apparently previously forgotten, to the lot of them.

"I do," Daisy said, fixing a cool expression on her face as she looked pointedly at her sister, who shrugged her shoulders and then followed Daisy out of the room, leaving it silent for a moment, until the Johnson children began to chatter once more.

Nathaniel wished he hadn't watched her backside swing from side to side as she walked out the door. He wished he could push the image of her gaze upon him out of his mind. But damn it, something about the woman had a hold on him.

Since he had joined the war effort, Nathaniel had one focus, and one focus only — to battle Napoleon and his forces. He had known that he would marry eventually, though at the time he hadn't known that his future wife would also become a duchess, making the requirement to wed even greater.

But now he was suspended in between responsibilities. The war effort was behind him, apparently no longer needing him. The home effort, which he was sure would prove to be considerable, was just out of reach, held in trust for him for a time while he was considered "missing" by most of his country, with only a select few knowing the truth.

It was that gap, he was sure, that had allowed thoughts of this woman to enter. Nathaniel finally picked up his soup spoon as he vowed that he must be rid of those thoughts — and fast — before he did something he would regret.

6

Nathaniel closed his eyes, reveling in the sound of the ocean swells around him as he sat on the beach the next morning. He had finally taken his own advice and left the confines of the inn, despite his fear that he would become stranded somewhere in the town without any method to make his way back.

But so be it. Far better to spend an entire day elsewhere within Southwold than trapped inside the inn once more.

The youngest girl, Violet her name was, had suggested he take a walk near the sea. At first, Nathaniel had dismissed her idea, as he felt he had seen more than enough shores in his lifetime; what was one more?

He was glad, however, that his feet had decided for him. The road next to the inn naturally led down to the water at a slight descent, and he easily followed the gentle slope down. The scent of saltwater drew him, while the breeze off the ocean and the sounds of its waves kept him there. He might have seen many oceans, but no beach had ever looked quite like this. It was the peacefulness of it that set it apart, he realized as he sat in the sand, removing his boots and stockings so he could feel the warm stones between his toes. He thought of the last time he had felt the earth upon his feet, and his memory flashed back to soldiers shouting, battles waging, the sound of guns firing and swords clashing around him — memories he wanted to remove rather than allow back into his consciousness.

But perhaps this moment, void of people and rather filled with only the gulls and the crabs likely lurking beneath some of the rocks nearby, could bring about a type of healing.

He eased his way onto his back, removing his jacket in the warm sun and placing it under his head in a pillow of sorts. Nathaniel wasn't sure how long he lay there, enjoying the moment, but when he heard footsteps approaching through the sand behind him, he sat up and whirled about, reaching for the weapon at his side that was only there in his memory.

Daisy stood still behind him, her hands raised in front of her as though she were guarding herself.

"Careful now," she said, lowering her hands and cautiously walking toward him. "I was only walking by and I didn't see you until the last moment. I'm sorry to have bothered you."

With a swish of her muslin skirts the color of the sky overhead and a billow of her cloak the color of the sand, she kept walking past him down the beach, but something made him call out to her, telling her to stop.

"Daisy!" he shouted over the sounds of the waves, and she turned back toward him, her eyes wide in surprise.

"Ah, Miss Tavners," he amended as she returned to him, standing in front of him as though in wait for whatever it was he had to say. Though the truth of it was, he really had nothing in particular he needed of her. He simply... wanted some company, even if it was her. The truth of it hit him fiercely, and he was only glad she had no way of knowing what he was thinking, for it not only sent a slice of pain through him, but was also rather embarrassing.

"Can I help you with anything?" she asked, but he was momentarily distracted by the dark tendrils of hair that had escaped her chignon and were now flying around her unadorned head. "Would you like a hand?"

Nathaniel simply grunted at her suggestion that he might need help, and he waved her offered palm away. He was *not* going to rely on a woman to help lift him from his position on the ground. He might be weakened some, but he was not completely helpless.

"Sit with me," he commanded, and she crossed her arms over her chest, quirking up one eyebrow. Nathaniel sighed and rephrased his request. "Miss Tavners, would you be so kind as to please sit with me a moment?"

She cocked her head to the side as she considered him, but finally good manners — or perhaps curiosity — prevailed, and she relented.

"Very well," she said. "But just for a moment. I have much to do."

"And what keeps you so busy today?" he asked, looking out at the ocean instead of at her, for he was too afraid that he would like what he saw. Why, he had no idea. Her younger sister — Iris, he thought — was much more of a classic beauty, with the curves to match. But there was something about this one that spoke to him, something he couldn't quite put his finger on. Perhaps he was too accustomed to battle and therefore was enjoying her contrary manner.

"The usual," she said with a shrug. "The markets for tonight's dinner, a quick visit with my friend Millie at the blacksmith's, and then returning home to clean and prepare said dinner."

"You do this, day after day?" he asked, hardly able to imagine such an existence.

"I do," she confirmed. "It is what most do, Mr. Hawke, as the majority of people have to work for a living."

He snorted. "I understand that. I am not an idiot."

"Well, what do you do, then? Clearly you are from some wealth."

He nodded slowly, unsure of how much to tell her. Part of it was keeping enough of his life a secret so as to not betray the army, the other was a question of how much he wanted to open himself up to her.

"My family does have some money, it's true," he said slowly, "However, I myself, as you know, was a soldier. Am a soldier."

"This was how you were injured."

"It was," he nodded.

"What happened? Where were you?"

Once again, Nathaniel paused for a moment as he was unsure of how to share the story. The truth was always easiest, but he would keep to the truth without any details.

"We were in France," he began, seeing images begin to flash before his eyes, this quiet, peaceful beach suddenly becoming a battlefield in front of him, men barreling into one another, the sounds of swords clashing against each other and the boom of firing cannons filling his ears. The smell of gunpowder and the scent of blood permeated his senses, and he closed his eyes to try to block it all out and focus on what he was telling her. He cleared his throat.

"We were fighting Napoleon's forces. It was a bloody battle, one in which both sides were determined to come out victorious, no matter the cost. I was... distracted, and was approached from behind. The man sliced through my calf. My legs buckled underneath me. I fell, and as I did I must have hit my head. The next thing I can remember, I was off the battlefield and in a cot upon the ground just beyond the battle. Apparently, I was out of consciousness for quite some time, for my fellow soldiers carried me to the trenches, where I was for who knows how long before they could move me. I was told my head would be fine, but my leg… well, the doctor wasn't entirely sure what would become of it."

Finally, he risked a glance over to Daisy, who was listening with her eyes wide.

"I'm sorry that happened to you," she said, and for once, her voice was filled with sincerity. "I cannot imagine the pain."

"At the time, I hardly noticed it. It's later, when the infection begins to set in, along with the realization that you will never be the man you once were — that's when the pain really begins."

"I can see how you would feel that way," she said, and then surprised him by placing a hand on his knee as she leaned into him, intent with the words she spoke. "But you must understand that compared to many, you were lucky. There have been men from our village — boys really — who have gone to fight and never returned, losing their lives in the process. Or there are men who are completely scarred or have lost entire limbs. Surely that would be worse."

"Of course it would," he said abruptly, jerking back away from her. "Do you not think that I have seen all of that, lived through it?"

"I never suggested you didn't," she said, removing her hand, placing it back in her lap. "I was only trying to remind you of what you still have."

The fact that it was hurt rather than her typical anger lacing her words at his reaction caused guilt to course through Nathaniel, but he wasn't entirely sure how to apologize for lashing out at her.

"I, ah, I didn't mean..."

"You are upset," she said carefully, her voice returning to its practical manner. "Which you have a right to be. War is a horrible thing, and often the very cause is not worth the sacrifice."

"In this instance, it is — to keep France's little Emperor from taking over the rest of Europe."

"Of course," she said softly, and he nodded, anxiety filling him at his helplessness, that he was sitting here on this damn beach when he should be doing something else to fight.

"What are you doing here?" she asked suddenly, almost as though she could hear his thoughts.

"Your sister suggested the beach would be a nice place to visit," he said, deliberately misunderstanding her question, hoping she would drop it.

"No, I mean here, in Southwold. Most of our guests are here because they are visiting nearby family, or come in the warmer seasons because they want to spend time near the ocean. Some are passing through for one reason or another, usually staying no more than a night. But you — you are just here."

He chuckled, evading her question. "Let me guess — you want me to leave?"

"You worry me."

"I'm not sure I understand."

"No one has any idea who you are or what you are doing here. You act as though you are a man who expects those around him to treat him with deference — but why? You were a soldier. You should be used to looking after yourself, should you not?"

He smiled slightly. He had been high enough in the army that there were others assigned to see to his needs, though he didn't often utilize their services for there was much else to be done.

"I suppose you have the right of it."

She stared at him with some consternation.

"You're really not going to tell me anything about yourself, are you?"

"On the contrary," he said. "I can tell you many things. I enjoy dancing — or I did, before this injury. I enjoy a good game of whist, though I despise faro. I have a sister who I adore. And I think very soon I will see about getting a dog."

"You are mocking me, sir."

"I am doing no such thing. I am telling you about myself, my life. Before you ask, I am not married because I knew I wanted to fight and had no wish to leave a wife behind."

Her cheeks colored at his words. "I never asked."

"You did not, but I knew you wondered all the same," he countered, enjoying seeing her flustered. "Now I ask you — where is your husband? You are well past the age of marriage, are you not?"

"That is rather rude," she said, her irritation turning to what was nearly anger.

"I thought we were being candid with one another."

"Very well, then, Mr. Hawke," she said, narrowing her eyes at him. "Do you want to know the truth of it? I also thought I would be married by now. In fact, all over the county, it was thought that I would be married to Lord Stephen Carter, Baron of Mansel, who is our local noble. At the time he was not yet the baron, but of course, he was always going to be."

"And then...?"

"And then his father passed, and the family's closest friends came to visit following the mourning period, including the Darlington family. Stephen was suddenly quite taken with Lady Almira Darlington, and upon the urging of their mothers, he found that she would make a much better baroness than the daughter of an innkeeper."

"I see," he murmured. Her story was short, all of the emotion omitted, but even with those few words, fNathaniel now had a better understanding of why she was so surly, untrusting, and not particularly pleasant when it came to her opinion of men or the nobility — both of which he was now decidedly a part.

"If you ask me, I think you should be grateful to Lady Almira."

"Grateful?" she looked at him incredulously.

"If it wasn't for her, you could now be married to the bounder, and he doesn't sound as though he is the sort of man to whom you would want to be tied for the rest of your life."

"I am surprised at you, Mr. Hawke," she said with raised eyebrows. "I thought you would defend Lord Mansel."

"Why?" he shrugged. "Because I am a man, myself? Did he, or did he not, Miss Tavners, provide you with the impression that he would marry you?"

"He most decidedly did."

"Then I remain within my original stance," he said with a nod. "For a man may have his fun, but to commit and then renege, that is unforgivable."

Nathaniel most often saw this type of behavior when it came to men who signed on to fight, believing in the romanticism of it all, but then they backed out the moment they saw blood. He supposed it was the same type of thought in this instance.

"Well," she said, looking down, apparently unsure how to respond to him now that he was on her side rather than arguing against her. "I best be going. Do you... need a hand?"

"I do not."

He did, but he would never admit it, especially to her.

"Very well. I shall see you later today. Good day, Mr. Hawke."

And with that, she stood, much more gracefully than he certainly would, and began to all but run down the beach, her blue skirts and buff cloak blending in with the shore surrounding her.

7

Daisy was most decidedly flustered. And she didn't like it — not one bit.

"Oh, Millie, I don't know what I was thinking, but the story just... came out!" She said to her friend during her quick stop at the blacksmith's, made shorter due to the time she had spent with Mr. Hawke. Why she had stopped, she had no idea. "What would possess me to share with Mr. Hawke the story that had caused me to be the laughingstock of Southwold for a few months?"

"I wouldn't say you were the laughingstock," Millie said kindly. "Lord Mansel was also not seen in a particularly good light."

"Either way, we were both certainly on the tongue of the town gossips for some time. Along with the discussion of the beauty of Lady Almira. For no one could deny that her looks were what turned his head."

"You are just as beautiful," Millie said with a smile.

"You must say that because you are my friend," Daisy sighed. "However, I thank you nonetheless."

"How interesting that this Mr. Hawke, who you claim to

be so surly and such a pest, came to your defense," Millie said, raising her eyebrows as she turned from her task of cleaning her father's shop to look at Daisy.

Daisy simply shrugged.

"I was rather taken aback as well."

"I can hardly wait to meet him myself," Millie said, turning her full attention on Daisy now. "I hear he is rather handsome."

A sick feeling filled Daisy's belly. She wasn't— no, she couldn't be *jealous* of her friend's interest in Mr. Hawke? Of course not. She was simply looking out for Millie, that was all. Besides that, her friend was already smitten with her fisherman, Burt.

"He may be a good-looking man, that much is true," Daisy replied. "But for one, he is altogether mysterious. No one knows how long he will be here, nor what he is actually doing here. It is suspicious."

"Perhaps it has something to do with his war effort," Millie said diplomatically, and when Daisy raised her eyebrows, Millie threw up her hands. "Yes, I know! I will side with you, Daisy. And I will be wary of the gentleman until he proves himself to us otherwise. It's only that you have been overly cautious since Stephen. Perhaps it is time you gave another man an opportunity."

"I am fine with my life as it currently is," Daisy said. "Besides, who would look after the inn?"

"Your parents — the owners?" Millie suggested, beginning what had long been an argument between them, for Millie felt that Daisy's parents placed far too heavy a burden on Daisy's shoulders. Millie may somewhat have the right of it, but Daisy didn't mind managing most of the duties at the inn. It kept her busy, and she liked keeping her hands and her mind occupied.

"Yes, but they need help. They are not young anymore."

"Then they should hire help."

"They cannot afford it."

"Which I do not entirely understand."

Daisy sighed. "Nor do I, Millie, to be honest, but my father is hardly forthcoming with that information."

"He shares the burden but not the information?"

"Millie..."

"I'm sorry, Daisy, I can't help but be protective of you," Millie said, placing her hands on the countertop in front of her. "Very well. On to other things. Have you chosen a dress for tomorrow evening?"

"Tomorrow?"

"For the dance!" Millie exclaimed.

"The one at *Stephen's* house?" Daisy asked with a bit of a laugh, "Oh, I will most certainly not be in attendance."

"But you must!" Millie protested. "All of Southwold will be there!"

"Except me."

"Daisy..."

"Millie. I am sorry, but I just cannot bring myself to go. To have everyone look between me — alone — and Stephen with his bride? There is much I can face, but not that. Please don't make me."

"Very well," Millie said with a sigh. "But you know I shall miss you."

"See that you do," Daisy said with a laugh. "Well, I really must be going. It was lovely to see you."

"And you."

With thoughts swirling in her head of tomorrow's dance, including wondering whether Millie and Mr. Hawke would get along, Daisy emerged from the blacksmith's shop into the bright daylight, blinking her eyes rapidly as she hurried to get back to her duties.

She had much to do, which certainly didn't leave time for fanciful thoughts such as these.

WHILE WALKING along the beach and through the town of Southwold hadn't exactly rid him of his boredom and his need to be active, at the very least it cleared his head and allowed Nathaniel to feel a little less closed in than he had previously.

He did the same the next day, though he found himself alone on the beach this time. He tried to deny the fact that he actually felt a bit bereft without Daisy's presence, but he supposed this was what happened when one was alone for too long. Instead, his mind turned to the battlefront, as he wondered if the army had managed to yet begin the strategy based on the plans he had stolen. He hadn't heard anything, but then, news often took a long time to reach English soil.

When Nathaniel returned to the Wild Rose Inn, his mind was working feverishly, and he asked Tavners for a pen and paper. He might not be able to do anything himself, but at the very least he could keep his mind fresh, could he not?

Nathaniel became so engrossed in writing out what would be his own battle strategy that he hardly noticed what was happening around him. When the eldest Johnson daughter stumbled into him with a quick, "Sorry, Mr. Hawke!" he finally looked up and saw she was running into another room with fabric in her arms, pieces of it trailing behind her.

It was only then that he realized he hadn't seen the

Tavners sisters in some time, and Mrs. Johnson flew through the shared sitting room wearing what he assumed was her Sunday best.

When they were called for supper an hour earlier than usual, he knew something was amiss. Then three of the Tavners sisters came in to serve wearing intricate hairstyles, ribbons, and smiles of anticipation — though still in their working dresses — and he realized he had clearly missed an invitation, not that he had been looking for one.

He took what had become his place at the table, addressing his question to Mr. Johnson.

"What is happening?"

Johnson looked at him in surprise.

"No one told you?"

"I do not believe so."

"There's to be a dance tonight at the home of our local gentry. All in the town are invited. It's a semi-annual event. I'm not sure whether it is to show off their wealth or because they feel they are giving back to everyone else in the village, but one thing is for sure, it's always a good time, and provides local gossip for months to come."

Johnson laughed at his own words, and Nathaniel snorted slightly in return. He had been to his share of such events. They could be fun, though they could also be rather... stilted. He hadn't lied to Daisy, however — he did love to dance. Not that he could at the moment.

Daisy herself walked through the door as Johnson was finishing his explanation, carrying a flask of red wine. Unlike her sisters, her hair was in its usual practical style, and she wore no ornamentation. She certainly didn't seem to be looking forward to anything.

Nathaniel quickly put the pieces of the puzzle together. A dance at the home of the local gentry, which Daisy didn't seem to be attending. It must be hosted by her former love.

"Not attending yourself this evening, Miss Tavners?" he asked with a raised eyebrow, and she shook her head with an air of nonchalance.

"I am not. Someone needs to look after things here."

"Oh but Miss Daisy, we are all attending," Mrs. Johnson said to her with affection. "You may as well come along."

"I will be here," Nathaniel offered, knowing it would leave her with a dilemma — attend with her family or stay here alone with him?

"I'm sure you are more than welcome to come along, Mr. Hawke," Mrs. Johnson said, her friendly face creasing in a smile. "Lord and Lady Mansel would have had no idea that you were staying within the inn."

"Besides, Mansel is always looking for a chance to impress someone new," Johnson said with a snort, clearly not a fan of the baron.

"Michael!" his wife admonished, though she was quite obviously hiding a smile of her own.

Nathaniel shrugged. "Perhaps. I did not exactly bring evening dress clothes along with me."

"We're a small village," Mrs. Johnson smiled. "You do not require anything particularly extravagant. Why, the jacket you wore at our first dinner is finer than most garments I've seen around here."

Iris walked into the room as Mrs. Johnson was speaking, and she turned to Nathaniel with her hands clasped in front of her eagerly.

"Oh, are you attending tonight's dance, Mr. Hawke?" she asked. "We just realized we were remiss in sharing with you the invitation. We had thought Father would, but of course, he can be somewhat... absent-minded. Anyway, if you are able, we would enjoy your attendance very much."

Nathaniel considered her words for a moment, then decided he certainly had nothing else to do, so why not see what this was all about? "Very well, I shall attend. And then, Miss Daisy, you will have no reason to stay home."

"Oh, Daisy isn't coming," Iris said with a quick shake of her head as Daisy returned to the kitchens.

"Does not everyone attend?" Nathaniel asked, and Iris smiled at him as she shrugged.

"Everyone but Daisy."

Nathaniel turned the thought around in his head as he finished his meal. He shouldn't care about Daisy's actions and whether or not she attended a local dance — he really shouldn't. But the thought of her missing what was likely one of the few social events this town held all year due to the idiocy of one self-serving baron... it angered him, and he determined it was time to set things right.

Supper was over quickly as they all were eager to get on with the night, but Nathaniel lingered until Daisy re-entered the room — alone — to clear the dishes.

"Mr. Hawke," she said, looking confused. "Should you not be getting ready for the dance? Or do you require a valet?"

She quirked an eyebrow as she said the last words with a touch of sarcasm, and Nathaniel couldn't help but smile.

"I will prepare myself in due time — I am capable, despite what you might think."

"I am glad to hear it."

"Though I am disappointed to hear, Miss Tavners, that you will not be in attendance."

"I should hardly think that my presence should make any sort of difference to your enjoyment of the evening," she said as she turned from him to pick up another dish, though before she did, Nathaniel could see a pretty pink blush had begun to fill her cheeks.

"I am more disappointed in *you* than anything else, Miss Tavners," he said, and she whirled back around to face him, her gaze now taut in anger.

"Excuse me?"

"Do you, or do you not, consider yourself to be a woman of strong character?"

"I do," she said, and she was certainly displaying her physical strength as she hefted an entire tray of dishes in her sinewy arms, leaving Nathaniel to feel rather helpless, but he couldn't very well carry it all while walking with only one fully functional leg.

"Then why are you shying away from a party at the home of your former love? All you are doing is showing him that you miss him, that he has hurt you. Do not give your enemy power over you, Miss Tavners."

"He was not exactly my *love*," she muttered. "Nor would I call him my enemy. It is simply the thought of entering his home, of all the villagers seeing me there, reminding them of what happened... I have no wish to relive such a time in my life."

"Then do not relive it," he suggested, "But begin anew."

She looked at him with curiosity now, her brow slightly furrowed.

"Why do you care?"

Why did he care? It was a question Nathaniel put to himself even now as she asked it, and the truth was, he didn't have a proper answer. He supposed it was the fact that he despised injustice and would far prefer to see people fighting for what was right and true. The thought of a man like himself turning a woman such as Daisy Tavners into a victim who doubted herself annoyed him to no end. He might not be fighting a battle on the front lines, but this was one battle he could lead. And he had the strategy to do so.

"I care because I dislike seeing people wronged, and I know you have the ability to fight for yourself," he said resolutely. "Where is the woman I know, who has challenged me since the moment I set foot in this inn?"

That made her smile, and she set the tray down on the table before her — which pleased him to see, for, at the very least, it meant she was not running from this conversation but accepting his words.

"I suppose it does rather grate on me to see a man such as the Baron think himself so important simply because of his title," she said, her words making him a bit uncomfortable due to his own position — the one of which she had no knowledge. He quickly moved on to his plan of attack.

"Very well, then, here is what we shall do," he said with the full authority that came from being both a major-general as well as a nobleman. "Prepare yourself for the dance and I will await you in the sitting room. Then I will escort you myself — along with your family, of course, to keep things proper. I will help ensure that all are aware that you are not lonely or in need of the baron's company, but that you have found yourself quite enjoying life without him."

Daisy eyed him shrewdly. "I am somewhat concerned about just how you plan to go about doing so," she said, biting her lip. "But oh, very well. It might be worth it simply to see the expression on Lady Almira's face."

"That's the spirit," he said with a smile. "I look forward to our first dance."

8

Of course, he had forgotten that dancing, at the moment, was likely not a possibility.

Nathaniel had realized that fact the moment after the words had left his lips, but he brushed away the thought, determining that it was of no consequence. He enjoyed dancing, but it didn't overly matter that he wouldn't be able to participate in this country affair.

At least, that's what he thought until he saw Miss Daisy Tavners enter the sitting room.

He had been aware of her attractiveness, despite the claws that were wont to come out when she was upset — which it seemed she often was when it came to him. He had never, however, seen her in anything but a worn muslin work dress, nor her hair in any style other than a severe chignon tied at the back of her head.

Tonight... tonight, she had transformed. Her dress was of a beautiful pale lavender, which softened her hard countenance, and instead of being pulled back away from her face, her dark hair was ever so slightly curled, with soft tendrils escaping the loose chignon to frame her defined cheekbones. She wore no elaborate adornments, but it was better that way, for if she had, she would no longer be the woman Nathaniel had come to know over a few short days.

He swallowed hard as he stood at her entry, his weight on his right leg. He was glad anew he had convinced her to attend tonight, though now for an entirely different reason.

"My family impatiently awaits in the foyer," she said softly, looking somewhat embarrassed, though why, he had no idea. "We had thought to walk — are you able to, or should we ready a horse?"

"I shall be fine," he said immediately, before he even had a chance to think over what she had asked. He was certainly not going to make a fool of himself, riding while the women and children walked along beside him.

As she accompanied him along the corridor, she asked softly, "Have you thought of using a cane?"

"I have."

"But you prefer to go without, for you believe doing so would take away from your strength and masculinity," she stated astutely, and he wanted to deny her words, yet he knew the truth to what she said. Was he really so transparent?

"I'm fine," was his answer instead, and she nodded. It was the last opportunity the two of them had to speak alone with one another as they all walked to the dance, Daisy's sisters full of questions over what had changed her mind to attend, questions to which she did not provide an answer.

What seemed like ages later to Nathaniel's leg, though was really only minutes, they came to the outskirts of the town.

"It's a ways down this road," Mr. Tavners explained. "Where you can see the candlelight dancing in the distance."

Nathaniel could see it well, and he wondered if he would be able to walk what looked to be a quarter-mile without collapsing upon the ground. They were nearing the entrance when it felt as though his leg was going to fall from under him at any moment, and Daisy took his arm, providing a bit of steadiness.

"You are accompanying me, do you not recall?" she asked as he was about to wrench the arm back from her, to tell her that he did not require any assistance. But at her words, he nodded. Aching calf or not, he would play the part he had promised her.

Nathaniel was surprised at how many people could fill a room. He had seen many crowds before at the parties and balls he had attended, but this crush of people was different somehow. Voices were louder, dancing was more exuberant, and the familiarity of the people surrounding him was much more apparent. He smiled, considering that it would certainly be an interesting evening if nothing else.

"Daisy!" A young woman about the age of the Tavners sisters — just before and beyond their twentieth years, he imagined — came rushing over to greet her, though her gaze remained trained upon him. He was an outsider, and he knew, therefore, there would be much interest in who he was and what he was doing amongst them.

This girl was blonde, her green eyes boring into him in both interest and — perhaps a little attraction? He couldn't be entirely sure.

"Millie," Daisy greeted her. "How lovely to see you. May I please introduce Mr. Hawke, one of our boarders?"

"Hello, Mr. Hawke," Millie said with the slightest of dips into a curtsy. "It is lovely to make your acquaintance. I have heard so much about you from Daisy."

"I can only imagine," he said with a smile for Daisy, who blushed ever so slightly, causing him to grin even wider.

"And just what have you heard?"

This caused the little pixie to fluster as well, for clearly, she had not heard much that she could repeat to his face.

"I ah, heard you are recently returned from the front lines," she finally managed. "It is very brave of you to fight."

"Yes, well, it is important to do our part," he said, an ache filling him at the thought that he was currently doing nothing — but attending a country dance. How insignificant.

He sensed Daisy growing rather rigid beside him, and he followed her gaze to see that it was upon the couple emerging into the room as though they were royalty attending a grand ball. Millie placed her hand on Daisy's arm in apparent support.

"I suppose this is the Lord Mansel I have heard so much about?" he asked dryly, and Daisy nodded smartly, looking away from the couple now and into his eyes.

"Yes," she responded. "And the beautiful Lady Mansel."

Nathaniel tilted his head as he studied the woman. She was stunning on first glance, that was certain. Her hair was dark, more midnight than Daisy's deep chestnut — apparently Lord Mansel appreciated a certain type of woman. Her gaze zeroed in on him — or Daisy, he couldn't be completely sure which — and as they neared, Nathaniel noted the cat-like smugness that filled it, destroying any beauty she held with a countenance most unattractive. The Baron was much the same — good-looking on the surface, but his gaze held such haughtiness, his nose lifted so high, that it was difficult to take him seriously.

"Miss Tavners," Lady Mansel said once she reached them, her husband a step behind her, clearly not entirely pleased with the direction they had taken upon entering the room. Most faces were now trained upon them, Nathaniel could see, but he was pleased that Daisy kept her head held high despite the stares.

"How lovely to see you," Lady Mansel continued, her words dripping with honey. She was dressed in a gown not entirely fashionable but wrapped tightly around her waist, the bodice cut low to reveal a voluptuous bosom. The deep red fabric clung to her until it began to fall away at her hips, cascading to the floor. It was obvious she desired for all eyes to follow her, and the condescending way she looked at Daisy caused Nathaniel to nearly shake with ire. "Isn't it lovely, Stephen?"

"Daisy— that is, Miss Tavners," the man said with a curt nod. "I am... surprised to see you here this evening."

"Why?" Millie asked, apparently prepared to defend her friend, even if it was to the highest ranking man living within their town.

"It has been a great deal of time since Daisy was last within our family's home, that is all," he said, and the look he turned upon Daisy was one that said he would have preferred it had remained that way.

"I had every wish to attend this evening," Nathaniel cut in, "and I was adamant Miss Tavners accompany me for I knew the evening would be much more enjoyable with her companionship. Forgive me — I am Nathaniel Hawke."

"Mr. Hawke," the Baron said, studying him. "Welcome to my home. I am the Baron of Mansel."

"Yes, I am aware," Nathaniel said with a tight smile, not enjoying the man's pompous tone. He made a note to never introduce himself in such a way when he assumed his role as the Duke of Greenwich. "Thank you for having me."

"Well," Lady Mansel said between the tension radiating

from the two men, "How lovely you were able to join us this evening. Do save a dance for me, Mr. Hawke, won't you?"

She turned and led her husband away, though he threw a backward glance over his shoulder, expressing his disdain for the lot of them.

"That went well," Daisy said dryly, and Millie laughed at her friend.

"I actually thought it went better than expected," she said as a quadrille completed.

The music slowed to a waltz as the lord and lady found their way to the center of the dance floor while all looked on, many joining in after a moment.

A young man came over to ask Millie to dance, and she gratefully accepted, her admiration for him obvious by the way she didn't break her stare from his.

"He's a fisherman," Daisy explained in Nathaniel's ear, and he found that he quite liked her closeness, both physically and the fact that she was there to share with him small bits of information about this town. "Millie's father would far prefer that she marry the son of the apothecary, who is already beginning to take over his practice, but she cannot think of anyone but Burt, despite the fact he is from a family of little means and will always be struggling to earn a dollar."

"It's an interesting quandary, what will make one happy in life," he mused. He had never considered marrying for love. In his family, most marriages were an alliance of one sort or another. He had managed to stay away from it entirely by remaining at war and out of London, but he would have to face the idea sooner or later, particularly when he would return as a duke.

"This is true," Daisy agreed. "Some marriages that begin in love end quite unhappily, though others that begin without it can come together. Or it may all go horribly wrong. It's hard to know the correct path to take."

"Did you love the Baron?" he asked, and Daisy tore her eyes from the dance floor to look at Nathaniel for the briefest of moments.

"No," was all she said as she looked wistfully at the couples circling the floor.

"I would dance with you if I could," Nathaniel said apologetically. "Though I am afraid that I wouldn't be much but a pole the way I can currently move."

"You said you loved dancing," she responded. "We do not need to follow the steps — people could hardly stare at me any more than they currently are. Come, I am game if you are."

Nathaniel raised his eyebrows. He had no wish to look a fool in front of all these people, but then... it wasn't as though he would see any of them again following his stay with the Tavners.

"Very well," he said with a shrug. "If you are comfortable in doing so, then so be it."

She nodded and took his proffered arm, and he led her onto the dance floor, ensuring he didn't use her as a crutch but rather escorted her as a man should.

Then he turned, held out his left hand to clasp her right, fitted his right hand around her waist, and looked down to meet her aquamarine eyes. And he nearly fell over.

For nothing in his life had ever felt so right before.

9

Daisy's breath hitched in her throat as Mr. Hawke stared down at her, seemingly as incapable of moving as she. On the outskirts of her mind, she knew they must begin moving or would soon become the centerpiece of this dance. And yet...

She was caught. Caught in his gaze, in his embrace, in her own thoughts and desires created by his very touch. Somewhere deep within the recesses of her mind, Daisy was aware that this was ridiculous — this man was pompous, arrogant, and altogether far too sure of himself. Not a man to whom she should be attracted. Not a man with whom she should be enjoying this non-dance. And certainly not a man she should have any feelings for besides disdain.

But none of those thoughts could overcome the warmth his touch sent through her limbs to her very core. She couldn't have explained it if she tried, but there was something about Mr. Nathaniel Hawke at this moment that reached beyond the words they had exchanged and spoke to a part of her deep within. Never before had Daisy felt such an instant attraction to a man. And she never wanted to again, for she had no idea how she was supposed to respond.

He regained his wits first, which Daisy only noticed because he began to sway back and forth in time with the music, gently moving her along with him. She shook her head to clear the spell from it as she willed herself to move out of her own thoughts and return to the ballroom, her body thankfully responding on its own to his motions.

Once she began to move, he led her around the floor in a modified waltz, one with an odd pattern in which he didn't quite step, but shuffled along the floor. His lips began to curl up ever so slightly, and she raised her eyebrows at him.

"Enjoying yourself?" she asked, and he nodded.

"Actually, I am," he said with a slight bit of incredulity. "Not long ago I was wondering if I would ever be able to dance again. I may never return to my former elegance, but it seems that I must not be making too much a fool of myself, or I am certain you would have left me alone on the floor by now."

"I would never do such a thing," she said, shaking her head, and he slightly started, his widening eyes betraying his surprise at her remark.

"Truly," she insisted. "If I so desperately did not want to be embarrassed in front of these people then I never would have come in the first place. I do hope your opinion of me is not so low that you think I would leave a man alone in the middle of the dance floor, especially in a place where he is a stranger to most."

"That is... kind of you," he said, though Daisy could tell he was confused.

"You do not know me," she said quietly. "I realize that perhaps I have been rude to you, and I apologize for that. But please know I am not as horrid as you may think."

"I never thought you horrid," he said in an equally soft tone, though his lips then really lifted. "Annoying, yes."

If both her hands hadn't already been occupied, she would have playfully slapped him, but as it was, she could only part her lips and shake her head at him to show her disdain. And drat it all, if the corners of her mouth didn't begin to curl up into a smile, leaving the two of them to dance around the floor grinning at one another like fools.

What was this man doing to her?

They remained silent for the remainder of the waltz, which passed much quicker than most dances in which Daisy partook. The odd time when she glanced about her, she noticed that there were more than few interested gazes directed their way — she knew many would be due to Mr. Hawke's unfamiliarity with the lot of them as well as the mysterious nature of his background. But then there were those who were also interested in her, knowing what they did of her previous relationship with Lord Mansel and the fact that Mr. Hawke had not only practically escorted her here, but had taken her onto the dance floor soon upon their arrival.

It hadn't even crossed her mind that anyone would care that he walked — or danced — with a slight limp, until he said as much to her.

When the music of the waltz faded, Mr. Hawke held out an arm and began to slowly lead her off the dance floor, back toward her family. Her sisters were watching her expectantly, and Millie looked more than enthusiastic at the fact that Daisy had taken on the dance floor and all of the spectators. Her concentration was broken when Mr. Hawke nearly stumbled, and she turned to look at him with some consternation.

"Are you all right?" she asked, worried at how pale his face suddenly was.

"I am perfectly fine," he said, though he very clearly was not.

"It's your leg, isn't it?" she asked before they came within earshot of her family. "The dancing was too much for it."

"If I can't bloody well dance, then how I am supposed to do anything of any consequence at all?" he asked, and Daisy was taken aback by the frustration within his voice.

"I realize you are in pain and likely suffering renewed disappointment regarding your reduced mobility, but there is no need to be surly," she said matter-of-factly, and he halted for a moment, seemingly taken aback by her calm admonishment.

"I apologize," he said, surprising her. Mr. Hawke did not seem to be a man who would ever be sorry for anything. Guilt flashed across his face for a moment. "I suppose you are right. I am used to being a man of action, who relies on his body as much as his brain. Now everything has changed, and I am not handling it as well as I should."

"I am sure that you will learn to adjust to your set of circumstances," she said. "I'm actually not sure you will have much of a choice, so I would highly recommend it as the best option."

They had reached the side of the dance floor once more, and she looked around her for a moment before turning a shrewd gaze back upon him.

"Come, sit."

"I'm fine."

"Stop being stubborn. There are plenty of chairs in the corner. You can rest for a minute. Do not forget we will have a long walk home later tonight. Fortunately, you have some time to recover."

A look of panic crossed his face, for he had obviously forgotten their mode of transportation.

"It's your own fault," she admonished him. "Had you not been so stubborn, you could have ridden one of Papa's horses. Why did you not bring one of your own, anyway?"

"I could not ride well at the time of my arrival."

Once more he evaded conversation regarding anything about him before he had appeared at their inn. Daisy sighed. "I would suggest you borrow a horse from Lord Mansel, but I would be loath to ask him of anything. Even if we had no history between the two of us, asking a favor of a man such as him can only lead to him feeling that we should be even further indebted to him, as our wonderful, benevolent lord."

"When you say, 'a man such as him,'" Mr. Hawke said, "Are you referring to his character?"

"His character, his title, does it matter? In my experience, Mr. Hawke, it is all the same."

Beside her, he stiffened in the chair he had just assumed. "I'm not sure that's fair."

"No?" she asked, rounding to stare at him. "When you were in the army, Mr. Hawke, did those within noble families receive the best positions, the titles, the very command?"

He looked down to the floor for a moment. "At times."

"At times? All of the time. Tell me I'm wrong."

"I do not suppose you are."

"Exactly. And didn't that irk you? Were there not men within the army, perhaps men such as yourself, who would have been far better qualified but were not born of the proper rank?"

"Some, yes," he conceded, but then he continued. "I do have to say, however, Miss Tavners, that often those men you disdain of, they have received an education that allows them to take on roles of command. There are many other men with the army who cannot read, who would not have the appropriate knowledge of history nor of politics to strategize."

"That is true of many," she said, "Though not all. What of you, Mr. Hawke?"

"I am... I have been fortunate," he said, and now wouldn't meet her gaze at all. Despite the fact that he obviously no longer wanted to speak of this, Daisy was once again perturbed. Why wouldn't he tell her anything about himself? She had already been curious before, but the closer she came to him, the more she wanted to know, and yet he continued to pull away from her.

"Who are you, Mr. Hawke?" she asked, leaning forward, finding his brown eyes troubled. "And why are you here?"

He looked panicked for a moment until a voice cut between them, and Mr. Hawke looked up gratefully when another young man joined them.

"Miss Tavners, would you care to dance?"

It was Millie's fisherman. Obviously, he had been sent to ask her to dance as Daisy would pose no threat to Millie's own pursuit of him. Daisy was annoyed that she hadn't been able to obtain any further information from Mr. Hawke, but when she caught Millie's pleading look from across the room, she nodded.

"If Mr. Hawke feels comfortable with his own company, then I would be happy to," she said, and Mr. Hawke nodded.

"Of course," he said in obvious relief. "Please do."

Daisy provided him one last look telling him that this was not over, that she would find out his secrets eventually, and then rejoined the dance floor.

10

Aside from Daisy's questioning and the fact that he could no longer tear his eyes from her person, which somewhat disturbed him, most of the evening was actually quite enjoyable. Nathaniel had never attended a dance that was not created from a carefully cultivated guest list, and while appearances were still obviously a factor here, there was more to the countenance of these people — a sincerity he wasn't used to.

They were a community, and despite the gossip and the odd rivalry, they quite obviously cared for one another.

When the Tavners and Johnson families were finally ready to leave, Nathaniel hauled himself to his feet after another brief respite. He had found that as long as he took enough breaks, he was able to spend some of the evening on his feet.

"Are you sure you are all right?" Daisy asked in his ear as they left the estate.

"I am," he affirmed with a nod, flashing her a quick smile that he hoped would appease her. She didn't look convinced, but she also didn't argue with him, which he appreciated. If anything, she seemed to understand his need to fend for himself on his own terms.

Even so, he lagged behind the rest of the group, but for the first time, he somewhat appreciated his lack of mobility as it meant that he and Daisy, who waited for him, had a few moments alone out of earshot of the rest of them.

"If you'd prefer to go on ahead, no need to wait for the cripple back here."

"Do not call yourself that," she admonished him, and he gave a bit of a snort as he shook his head.

As much as he didn't want to admit it, his leg was sore, the place where the muscle had been sliced through now throbbing. He should be taking better care of it, he knew — it was not as though he had anything else to do, now did he?

"Have you spent much time in London?" she asked now, surprising him as they walked down the incline from the Mansel estate.

He supposed there was no reason why he couldn't answer that question.

"I have, actually."

"What's it like?" she asked now, turning her face up to him, her high cheekbones and sea blue eyes illuminated in the moonlight. He wasn't sure he had ever seen anything more beautiful.

"London?" he asked, attempting to shake himself from his trance. "You've never been to London?"

"I've been once, with my father," she said, a wistful look coming over her face. "He had meetings there, and I convinced him to take me along. But I didn't see much of the city. Nothing really beyond the inn where we stayed and some of the marketplaces. I feel as though you must know another side of London — the fashionable side."

"I'm not sure as though I would call it *fashionable*," he said with a slight chuckle.

"As much as I know you don't want to share your life with me, I know you come from some wealth," she persisted. "That much is clear. What is it like? To ride a carriage through London, or to walk the huge parks surrounded by all manner of people and beautiful buildings?"

Nathaniel had never really thought much about those aspects of his life. They all had been just that — regular, everyday activities. He had been raised in the countryside during the summers and then would spend every Season with his family in London, where their manor was large enough to make Mansel's country estate look small in comparison.

"I suppose carriage rides are no different than most," he said with a smile in answer to her question. "The buildings are impressive to look at, though in a different way than what nature holds. The life itself can be interesting, depending on what you enjoy. If fashions and gossip and taking tea is enjoyable, then living in London — as a person with money — would be rather remarkable. I always far preferred to keep myself occupied and as a—" He was about to say as the son of a nobleman, but caught himself in time. "As a man without a title, I had little with which to keep myself occupied, and I had no wish to become one of those dandies who spends his days chasing women and his money on gambling and the like. That is why I joined the war effort, I suppose. I was bored."

"You were bored," she said incredulously as she stared off in the distance. Then she turned to eye him once more. "You haven't described the parks."

"The parks? Well yes, they are beautiful, but nothing can

compare to the country, in particular what you have here in Southwold, with the ocean on one side and what looks to be meadows and fields on the other."

"It is rather lovely when you think on it," she said, her head tilted ever so slightly to the side in a whimsical way. "Actually—" She stopped suddenly and raised a hand to point out into the inky darkness across the way. "Over there, you can't see it now, but just over the rise, there is a large oak tree in the distance. Surrounding it is a field of bluebells as far as the eye can see. It's quite beautiful and so incredibly peaceful. Sometimes, if I have a moment, I like to go sit right at the base of that tree, and just take in the beauty that surrounds me. Next to the beach, it's probably my favorite place in the world."

Suddenly she dropped her arm, and her head as well.

"I'm sorry, I became somewhat carried away, lost in my thoughts."

"There is nothing to apologize for," he responded gently. "It sounds beautiful. I'd like to see it."

"Truly?" she asked, her head turning toward him once again. "You, the man of action, want to see my peaceful, boring meadow?"

"It doesn't sound quite so boring, the way you describe it," he said with a grin.

"Very well," she said, and he could hear the self-consciousness in her tone. "Tomorrow we shall go. This time, we'll take the horses."

Last night, with only the moon for illumination and the night dark and still around them, riding to her oak tree, as she thought of it, had seemed like a marvelous idea. Today, Daisy was greatly regretting her decision.

She had only an hour or so before she would have to rush to the marketplace to gather supplies to begin creating tonight's dinner, but it would have to be enough time for Mr. Hawke.

Daisy would have told her father where they were going, but at the moment, he was nowhere to be found. She told Marigold instead, who looked at her with wide eyes.

"Are you sure you should be going riding with Mr. Hawke... alone?" Marigold asked, biting her lip, and Daisy shrugged her shoulders.

"He seems perfectly respectable, and he asked to see the countryside. Who else would take him?" Daisy questioned, though Marigold didn't look convinced.

"I'm surprised, following your initial reaction toward him. However, he does seem like a good, respectable man, but really, we do not know much about him at all," Marigold persisted.

Well, that much was true. They didn't know anything about Mr. Hawke, but as annoyingly arrogant he could be, she had no worries about him being anything but appropriate in their encounters.

"It will be fine, Marigold," she assured her sister. "Father seems to know him and has no concerns about him residing at the inn. We will return in less than an hour."

Marigold finally nodded, but still looked worried as Daisy gave her one last reassuring smile as she left the house to the stables next door to prepare horses for the two of them. They owned three, all of them being somewhat slow workhorses, whose main role was to pull their wagon if they had to travel some distance. But they were sturdy and dependable, which, quite honestly, was likely what Mr. Hawke needed at the moment.

"Good morning," he said, startling her as she prepared the tack, and Daisy couldn't help the smile that spread across her face at his voice. She couldn't understand why his very presence would bring her happiness when he had been so surly to her for so long, but she couldn't deny that being around him caused a sense of giddiness to fill her. It was embarrassing yet somehow… pleasant.

"Good morning," she responded, attempting to temper in her smile before she turned around, not wanting him to realize that she was actually somewhat looking forward to this outing.

"This is Lucky," she said, running a hand over the horse's smooth roan head, and Lucky nuzzled her neck in response, causing Daisy to laugh. When she looked up, Mr. Hawke was staring at her somewhat strangely, but Daisy lost track of her thoughts when Lucky whinnied into her neck once more.

"All right, boy," she said, reaching into her pockets and pulling out a sugar cube. "Here — enjoy. Lucky will be yours for the next hour," she said as she led him over to Mr. Hawke. "I'll ride Sally over here."

"Lucky and Sally?" he asked with a raised eyebrow as he greeted Lucky. "Not Lily or Pansy?"

"They were already named before my mother got to them," she said dryly, though she couldn't help but laugh. "I don't have much time, so we should be on our way. It won't take long to get there on horseback."

Daisy typically walked to the meadow, so on horseback it was but a few minutes. When they reached the little wood, she dismounted, smiling as she looked around at the place that had become her secret little corner of the world, the shimmering haze of blue-violet flowers emerging from their bright green leaves, spread across the expanse beneath the surrounding trees.

She closed her eyes for just a moment as she breathed in the sweet yet spicy scent of the bluebells, mixed with the smell of the rich earth beneath them and the cool air above. She smiled, allowing it all to invade her senses, for a moment washing away everything else that typically filled her mind — the lists of things to do, to buy, to prepare.

"This is stunning."

For a moment, she had nearly forgotten Mr. Hawke, and when she turned, he had dismounted himself and was standing with his hands on his hips as he looked about them.

"It is, isn't it? I found it one day when I was out walking and actually fell asleep right under that tree! And I never fall asleep in the middle of the day," she said with a self-conscious laugh. No, her mind was far too busy, her lists of tasks too long for time to sleep under a tree. But this area brought her peace.

"You won't find this in London," he said with a wink as he tied their horses to a tree branch, and she nodded.

"I suppose not."

Feeling somewhat vulnerable, she ventured deeper into the bluebells, allowing their beautiful violet petals and dark green leaves to cover the black of her boots. She had a crazy impulse to take her boots off and run through the field barefoot, but she certainly wouldn't do that in front of Mr. Hawke — would she?

"What is it?" he asked, sensing her pondering.

"It's just..." she felt silly even saying it aloud.

"What?"

"I wonder what it might be like to feel the softness of the plants on my toes."

He laughed and she blushed, for he was obviously astounded that she would even think such a thing. But then, to her surprise, he hobbled over to a tree stump, sat down, and took off his own footwear.

11

Nathaniel knew he was being ridiculous. But there was something about Daisy's infectious spirit, of this place which seemed magical, in a strange way. He had never been one for the whimsical nor the emotional — he was a man who set a purpose and followed through. Though that had been his opinion of Daisy as well, and here she was, releasing all of her cares in a meadow full of blue flowers.

He could tell she was embarrassed about her own reaction, and so he had done what he could to ease her worry — by joining her. He stood now, feeling the coolness of the soft flowers on his toes, and he followed her lead in closing his eyes to experience the sensations. When he opened them, she stood with bare feet, her boots discarded beside her.

She ventured forward a few steps, and then, just as the sunlight broke through the trees, she flung her arms out and spun in a circle, tilting her face toward the warmth filtering through the branches above her, and Nathaniel could only stand and stare at her in awe.

Never, in his entire life, had he seen anything so beautiful as the sight currently before him. He had seen the tragedies and horrors of war, and he had also seen plenty of artificial beauty in the dyed gowns, painted faces, and exquisitely coiffed hair of women as they twirled about dance floors. Buildings constructed in a wide variety of materials, painted scenes to resemble the very nature that lay around them had been part of his everyday life.

Daisy, however, in this woodland, was what was true, what was real. This image in front of him spoke to his very soul in a way nothing ever had before.

And he knew, deep within him, that his yearning for her was something he could no longer deny. He took tentative steps toward her, though what he was planning to do once he reached her, he had no idea. She made the decision for him, however, extending her arms, taking his hands in hers.

"Dance with me?" she asked, her face open and vulnerable, her voice somewhat pleading, as though she was concerned that he would say no, that she would be left alone in her exhibition of joy.

Nathaniel refused to allow that to happen. He took her hands, smiled, and danced as though there was no pain holding him back, no immobility that would keep him from enjoying this day, this moment, this woman.

Interestingly enough, without his boot rubbing against the back of his calf, his leg felt better than it had since the injury. He let go of the thoughts of all that had happened, all he had experienced, all he was missing, to simply enjoy this dance. The music was born of the blackcaps and nightingales chirping in the air around them, the wind rustling through the tree leaves, and the faraway sound of the ocean waves in the distance.

Finally, at the same moment, they began to slow until they stood, motionless, staring at one another as though they were the only two in the entire world.

Daisy's eyes were wide, searching his, and Nathaniel reached up to stroke her pale, satiny cheek with his thumb as his hand cupped the side of her head, his fingers threading through the silky strands of her hair that had come loose from her usual chignon.

She said nothing but leaned ever so slightly into his touch, and he took that as a sign of her willingness to want this in equal measure. He bent his head, pausing for a moment to provide her a chance to retreat, and then softly touched his lips to hers.

Daisy didn't disengage, but she was hesitant, and Nathaniel wondered if she had ever been kissed before. If she had, it didn't seem to be by anyone who appreciated what she had to offer. It pleased him, knowing that he would be the one to show her such a thing, for a possessiveness filled him as he held her, and the thought of any other man holding her or touching her in such a way caused extreme jealousy to fill him.

He pressed his lips harder against hers, deepening the kiss, his lips kneading hers. She may have been inexperienced, but it was clear that anything Daisy Tavners did, it was with full intention. She met the pressure of his lips, and when he touched his tongue against hers, she opened to him, shocking him and yet inexplicably pleasing him at the same time.

She tasted as sweetly spicy as the bluebells, like cinnamon, he thought, with a touch of sugar. He stroked the softness within her mouth, unable to explain the tenderness that came over him as he held her. Her tongue, often so tart and so accusatory — particularly toward him — was now sending sensations of heat and appreciation throughout his body. He had to stop this before it went too far, he told himself, as he fought an internal battle over whether or not he should pull away. If he continued, they might find themselves on the floor of this meadow, and he was not that kind of man, one who would take a woman's innocence and then leave her behind.

For he was, as difficult as it still was to believe, a duke now, and in time he would be returning to London and his estate near Chelmsford with new responsibilities, while she would remain here, in Southwold, tending the inn with her family. Suddenly the thought of Daisy, clothed in the finest of gowns as she walked into a ballroom on his arm, filled his consciousness, startling him so much that he rather brusquely stepped back from her.

Daisy stared up at him, her eyes wide as she brought a hand to her lips, resting it against them as though she could hardly believe what had just happened.

"Mr. Hawke…" she said, her voice hardly above a whisper.

"Nathaniel," he corrected her. "I'm sorry…"

"Do not apologize," she ordered, fire now back in her eyes, which he couldn't help but appreciate. "That was… unexpected, but wonderful nonetheless."

He nodded, agreeing with her, and she finally broke her eyes away from his, looking around her at their surroundings. They were still alone, of course, but for the birds and the animals of the forest. How interesting that nothing around them had changed, while for him, everything seemed to now be different from what it was but moments ago. He swallowed, unsure of what else to say. He could hardly make her any promises, for she had no idea who he even was. Yet it seemed wrong to simply pretend this had never happened.

"Let's walk," she said, solving his dilemma, and he nodded, taking her offered hand and following her slowly through the meadow. She began to point out much of the flora around them, describing certain trees and plants, telling him when they bloomed and what they smelled like, what they would look like through various seasons.

"How do you know so much about all of this?" he asked her, and she shrugged.

"My sister is the one who truly loves all that nature has to offer. She knows it in a way that I don't. She understands what nature can give us, what we must, in turn, do for it. It is difficult not to remember some of the information she loves to chatter on about." She laughed. "I love the beauty it offers, the peacefulness. As does Marigold of course, but she also appreciates its usefulness."

There was something about this place, the conversation, the easy flow of it, that had changed Daisy, allowing Nathaniel to see her in a slightly different light. All the worries of her work at the inn — whether it be self-imposed, or placed upon her by her parents — flew away from her, and she was left the woman she would have been had she not had so many cares.

She looked up at him now, her face still relaxed, but her smile drifted away.

"How long will you be staying here with us?" she asked. Nathaniel could tell that she was feigning nonchalance but knew that her question likely held much more significance, especially after what had just happened between them. For that was no ordinary kiss, whether she was aware of it or not.

"I am unsure," he said, and as she turned away from

him, he could sense her frustration with him at not answering her. But for once, it was not that he was purposefully avoiding doing so — he truly didn't know. He hesitated for a moment before continuing, deciding he could trust her.

"I am here until I am told otherwise," he said. "I await orders."

She turned to him now, somewhat shocked.

"You are here because the army has sent you here?"

He nodded.

"Why?"

"I cannot entirely say."

"Of course."

She was silent for a moment. "I must offer you an apology, Mr. Haw— Nathaniel," she said, her gaze on the indentation of a path ahead of her. "When you first arrived, I was not particularly pleasant to you, I realize that. Your countenance was, however, rather..."

"Arrogant?" He chuckled. "I believe that was one word you used to describe me."

"Yes, well... you seemed to have quite a few expectations of those of us working at the inn. I know only one other man who treats people as such."

"Your baron."

"Lord Mansel, yes. I understand this is the way of things, 'tis true, but to be the one under orders is not particularly pleasant."

Nathaniel had never stopped to consider the thought, for those who worked for his family were well-paid and pursued the positions.

"Perhaps it is because you never asked to work in such a position as you currently do," he mused aloud.

"What exactly do you mean?"

"You didn't decide to build or own an inn. You didn't decide to spend your days and nights working there serving others. Your parents did. Do you get paid for the work you do?"

"Of course not, as my parents support me — and all of my sisters. How would they ever pay us?"

"Did they ever pay employees, when you were young?"

"A few, yes," she relented. "But we were just children."

"They are taking advantage of you, Daisy," he said, her given name falling from his tongue without thought.

"They are my parents!" she protested, waving an arm in front of her, emphasizing her point. "Besides, I like the work I do."

"Very well," he said, not wanting to break the peace they had found by furthering this argument. He had no idea how much time they would end up having together, and he didn't want to spend it in opposition.

"Speaking of which, we must return," she said, "for I must run to the market."

"I'll come with you."

"Are you sure? Do you feel up to hobbling amongst the stalls then?"

"Why not? I have never been to a marketplace before," he said, shocking her.

"Well then," she said with some laughter. "You're in for a treat."

He did, surprisingly, enjoy himself much more than he ever thought he would at the market. However he knew it wasn't because of the market but the woman who accompanied him. Daisy knew nearly every person there, both those who were selling their wares, and those who were shopping along with them. She efficiently greeted all of them and yet was not distracted from her purpose.

It was interesting watching her, and Nathaniel appreciated the fact she had allowed him to come along. And when they returned to the inn after their outing and parted ways, he realized just how much he wanted to remain with her.

12

Daisy had hardly slept a wink. Which she hadn't expected to — not after that kiss with Nathaniel. She relived it over and again in her mind, the pressure of his lips on hers, the taste of coffee on his tongue, the strength of his arms as they wrapped around her. Never had she thought that she would allow a man like Nathaniel to come close to her, but then, she had never truly met someone like him either.

He was a mystery, which, in the same breath, was intriguing and yet also quite annoying. She longed to know who he was, what kind of life he had left at home. Did he have a family? A house of his own? A— no, she wouldn't think it. He had told her that he hadn't left anyone waiting for him, and she believed him, for at the time, he had no reason to lie to her.

She groaned aloud as she dropped her head in her hands, and Marigold began to sit up groggily, bringing a hand over her mouth as she yawned.

"Goodness, Daisy, what time is it? And whatever has come over you?"

"Nothing. Nothing at all," Daisy said hastily, having no wish to tell anyone — even her sister, the person who was closer to her than anyone else in this world — what had happened yesterday in the meadow.

The fact that she had even shown him her patch of bluebells and the oak tree — the one place she had kept entirely to herself — should have been enough for him to open up a bit about himself, but alas, it was not to be. True, he'd told her some things about himself, but it was such a paltry amount he may as well have said nothing. She sensed that he'd wanted to share more, yet something was holding him back. Why the secrecy, she had no idea. What on earth could have happened in a battle across the sea against the French that would prevent him from sharing anything about himself with her family, or, in particular, with her?

She sighed as she flung back her blanket and began to hastily prepare herself for the day, which would begin with making breakfast for the boarders, followed by cleaning the rooms and tidying her family's quarters.

Daisy was bustling down the hall to the kitchens when the connecting door from the boarders' sitting room swung open, nearly hitting her in the face.

When she saw who it was — the very man who was occupying her every thought — she brought a hand to her breast and attempted to re-catch her breath.

"Nathaniel!" she exclaimed as he reached out, grasping her by the shoulders to steady her. "You startled me."

"My apologies, Daisy," he said regretfully. "But I cannot say that I am upset to meet you like this, for I was on my way to find you."

"Is something amiss?"

"Not at all," he said, dropping his hands. "I was actually

coming to see if you might like to walk with me to the shore before breakfast."

She stared at him incredulously. "A walk? Now?"

"Well, yes. The sun has just risen, and the weather is a perfect temperature."

"Breakfast must be on the table in but an hour!"

"We will return by then."

"Nathaniel... who do you suppose will *make* the breakfast?"

"Can your sisters not do it today?" he asked, his brow furrowing.

"No, I couldn't ask them to — it's not their responsibility, it's mine," she said, lifting her hands in the air. "They help, of course, but I cannot just leave them without any sort of instruction or idea of where to begin."

"It's just breakfast, Daisy," he said in disbelief.

"What may seem insignificant to you is part of my everyday life," she said, trying to maintain calm as she explained. "You have plenty of time available to do what you please, and that is perfectly fine. I can imagine that it must be altogether lovely. However, that is not my life, nor do I have it within me to simply leave my responsibility for a bit of fun."

His brown eyes darkened slightly, but he simply nodded and turned to the door.

"Very well, Daisy. Forgive me."

And then he was gone, the door swinging shut behind him, and all Daisy could do was sigh. Why, oh why, was he so contrary? It was as though he were two different men — charming in one moment, aggravating in the next. When he wasn't given his way, she realized, he became surly. He was used to receiving what he expected, which bothered her, for that was what she had never liked about Stephen.

There was one thing for sure. Daisy had to find out more about Mr. Nathaniel Hawke. Or whatever this was between them would be over before it even began.

~

NATHANIEL STEWED as he waited for breakfast, while he ate breakfast, and now, as he sat in the worn yet surprisingly comfortable leather chair looking out the front window at the empty street beyond.

It wasn't so much Daisy's denial that caused him chagrin. No, it was the fact that her words brought about guilt deep within his soul. For while she spoke of breakfast, he had responsibilities of his own — those he had left behind on the warfront, and those that awaited him at home, while he sat here doing nothing.

There were dual thoughts running through him at the moment. So much inside of him longed to return somewhere he was needed, where he could take action to help a cause. And yet, that would also mean leaving Daisy. It perplexed him, how after only a few short days he could feel so tied to her. He knew this could be nothing more than a short flirtation, but when he thought of never seeing her again, regret filled his soul.

He sighed, rubbing at his temples, but looked up when there was a knock at the door and it slowly creaked open. He forced a smile on his face when Daisy walked in, her expression hesitant.

"Nathaniel? You have some correspondence. Iris was going to bring it to you, but I thought perhaps we could speak once more. I never meant any offense earlier this morning. I realize you are likely not used to the workings of an inn, nor what is typically involved or my own responsibilities."

Nathaniel tapped the envelope on his knee, longing to open it, for a quick glance at the front of it revealed General Collins' heavy scrawl. Yet he equally wanted — no, *needed* — to speak with Daisy.

"I would like to apologize as well," he said. "The truth is, your words only reminded me of all that I am neglecting while I am here."

She looked at him expectantly with eyebrows raised, and he knew what she wanted. He would determine what he was able to tell her, he decided — *after* he read the contents of this envelope.

"When you have a moment — whenever that may be," he said, "Why do we not walk then, and I will answer your questions?"

He saw the gleam come into her eyes then, and she nodded curtly. "Two o'clock?"

"Two o'clock," he said with a wink, and she blushed slightly before one of the Johnson children pushed open the door behind her, nearly knocking her over, though she only laughed, clearly used to chaos, before shutting the door behind her.

Nathaniel greeted the child before ripping open the seal at the back of the letter, releasing its contents to his eager eyes. It was dated a week prior, which somewhat aggravated him, for situations changed so quickly on the front.

Major-General Huntingwell,

I am pleased to inform you that the intelligence you provided is proving to be most useful. I will have more information in a few days once we execute the attack we are planning. After that time,

I will contact you as regards your release to return to London. Do not be a stubborn fool, and use your cane.

Sincerely,

General Collins.

No further information, then, besides the fact that he should soon be released from the inn to return, though not to the war effort, but to London. Where he would assume his role of duke, heaven help him. He knew of no man who would turn down such a title, yet he was unsure whether he was prepared for it. Most gentlemen would spend years learning from their fathers before assuming such a role. But he supposed if he could command military forces, he could oversee a few estates, could he not?

He wasn't sure what he could tell Daisy, either. He wanted to trust her, to tell her all, and yet... he was also fearful of how she would react. For if she knew he would not only be returning to London, but returning to inherit a ducal title, she might reject him altogether, and she was now the only aspect of this stay that was making it bearable. After her experience with Lord Mansel, he knew she was left with ill taste regarding the nobility, and he would prefer that she came to know him better as a man before she was aware of him as the Duke of Greenwich.

As for what would happen with the two of them... they were just beginning to explore their growing connection to one another. He felt sick at the thought of leaving her with hardly any explanation — but he wasn't sure just what else he could do.

13

Nathaniel was pleasantly surprised when Daisy sought him out prior to the time they had arranged. She had already provided him with strict instructions to not eat a mid-day meal, and he now understood why, as she carried a picnic basket over her arm. Despite her attempts to dissuade him, he took it from her as they departed the inn. She hardly said a word to him in her rush to bustle out the door.

"Are you running from something?" he asked, trying not to laugh at her, and she shot him a look.

"My sisters," was all she said by way of explanation, and sure enough, she was unsuccessful in her endeavor.

"Have fun!" they heard Iris call, and Nathaniel turned to see the young woman's impish grin following them as they walked down the road. All three of them had gathered at the door, wearing expressions varying from confusion to hopefulness, though why, Nathaniel was unsure. He hoped the family was not expecting too much from the time he and Daisy spent together, for he was unaware of what potential outcomes there could be.

Daisy pointed out various shops within the village, said hello to passersby and kept a pace that Nathaniel knew was for his own benefit as they continued on their way.

"I know the perfect picnic spot," she told him, and sure enough, they slowed when they neared a small stretch of grass just behind the sandy shoreline, slightly secluded from the road beyond so that they wouldn't be within eyesight of all meandering this far down the road.

Nathaniel spread the blanket upon the grass and held a hand out to help her sit down upon it. She eyed him as though she thought he was likely the one who needed some assistance in easing himself down, but he was relieved when she finally accepted his hand with a smile. Nathaniel was starving, and, knowing how capable Daisy was in the kitchen, had to restrain himself from diving into the picnic basket like an animal.

"Did you prepare our meal?" he asked.

"I did," she said, and he could have sighed when he saw all that she had packed now spread out before him on the blanket.

"Thank you," he said before immediately biting into the chicken leg he had found within the basket. "I have never been to a picnic quite like this before. Certainly not one with so great a feast. And never one with a woman like you."

She eyed him. "What is that supposed to mean?"

"Nothing but what I said — I have never met a woman like you before, Daisy, and that's a good thing," he said honestly, realizing the truth of his words as he spoke. "You work hard, but you do not complain about it. You do so to allow others to find pleasure and happiness within their own lives. Because of all you do, your sisters are able to spend their time doing what they enjoy — Marigold with her potions and powders, Iris with her friends in the village,

Violet with her books. Your mother can then spend her time gossiping and fretting about all around her, and your father can do what he does best — nothing. You take all the burden, sharing it with no one."

Daisy's eyes turned somewhat stormy as he spoke, taking Nathaniel aback.

"Is that what you truly think of my family?" she asked, her voice low, just above a whisper. "That none of them have any redeeming qualities?"

"Of course they do!" he exclaimed. "Daisy, I was only telling you what I admired about you."

"And in doing so you question the character of the people who are the very closest to me?"

Nathaniel sighed. He had apparently been too long away from society, for it seemed he had utterly forgotten how to make polite conversation with a woman. "I didn't mean it that way. I know they help you, Daisy, I do, and they have all been nothing but friendly and welcoming since I came to stay at the inn. It is only... I suppose it concerns me that you seem to take on the burdens for all."

"When you say they all have activities they enjoy, the truth is, Nathaniel, I *enjoy* being the one in charge, telling others what to do, doing what I can myself. Besides a walk in the meadow or at the seashore, there is really nothing else that I do for a pastime. I like to be busy."

Nathaniel nodded in understanding. And then suddenly, a vision filled his mind. One of Daisy, the woman who enjoyed control, busyness, and the managing of all around her fitting perfectly into the role of Duchess, in which she would oversee the households, the servants, the social events, and the family. Which would make her... his wife.

The thought took him by such swift surprise it nearly

took his breath away.

If he remained Nathaniel Huntingwell, son of the second son of a duke, then perhaps it wouldn't have been an issue. But as the Duke of Greenwich... he had an idea of the world he would be entering, and even with his upbringing, he was somewhat fearful of what the future held for him. To bring Daisy in with him... he had no idea of how she might react. Whatever was between them might be finished before it had hardly even started.

And yet...

"I suppose I just want to see you happy," he mumbled, and her eyes widened.

"I am happy."

"Are you?"

"Of course."

"Are you happy to be here with me?" he asked, shocking himself with the question, for it exposed his vulnerability — a side that he had always ensured he kept well hidden.

"I am," she said, her cheeks turning bright pink, though she didn't break eye contact with him. "I almost hate to admit it, but I am. Nathaniel... I need to know more about you, however, or else I risk allowing you to hurt me, and I do not wish to be hurt again."

"Damn Mansel," he muttered, but Daisy shook her head.

"To be honest with you, I never felt much for him at all," she said. "I believe it was more so that he, the most powerful of all the villagers, was interested in *me*. There was never any thought that I would ever refuse his attention, until I came to know him better and realized just how arrogant he was, how he thought he was above us all. What actually hurt most was to be tossed carelessly aside so suddenly the moment he saw Lady Almira, as though there had never been any promise between us at all."

She shrugged. "After that, I decided that perhaps I was not the kind of woman who would welcome another chance at marriage."

"Did you not think you could find a love match?" he asked, suddenly needing to know the answer to this more than any question he had ever asked before.

She kept her eyes down, seemingly intent on stirring the pudding she had removed from the basket.

"Similar to what Millie is hoping for? Honestly, I'm not entirely sure. My sisters would love if I were to marry, of course, for then they think others would be more inclined to pursue them. However, it is not as though many other men have shown any interest in me — at least, not the serious type — so I'm not entirely sure why my sisters would suppose such a thing could ever happen."

Nathaniel followed her gaze as it strayed away from him, and he reached out, placing a hand on her knee, which she looked at for a few moments before returning her gaze to his face.

"Men are intimidated," he said, staring at her intently, needing her to understand the truth of what he spoke. "Many men are interested in a woman who will only do as they say, which I do not quite understand. If a woman is able to take control, that would provide the man with much more freedom to do as he wished."

"So what of you?" she asked, cutting through his compliments to the heart of the matter. "Do you have a woman waiting for you at home, ready to share command with you?"

He could tell she was attempting nonchalance, but her eyes kept darting up toward him. Nathaniel not only enjoyed the way she phrased her words, but also the jealousy behind them — for it meant she cared.

"I do not," he assured her.

"Did you ever?"

He shrugged. "There have been interested women before, but I always had more to do first — such as contributing to the war effort. I did not want to leave behind a woman who would have to wait for me, wondering if perhaps I would ever come home."

"But home you will go."

"Home I will go." He nodded.

"And where is that?"

"Partially in London. Partially near Chelmsford."

"You have a country estate, then?"

He would have more than one estate once he returned, but he didn't think that was the best place to start in his explanation.

"My family does," he explained, deciding to stay with what was, for the most part, the truth. "We are wealthy, it is true, and... we do have noble blood within the family, though my father is without a title."

Nathaniel stopped for her reaction, but Daisy just remained sitting, waiting for him to finish his explanation, which he actually appreciated.

"I spent my life with my parents attending society events, hosting them sometimes. My father enjoyed the racetrack, so I spent a great deal of time there with him. Eventually, I suppose I became bored. I was educated at the finest schools, but not for any particular purpose. I had no wish to become a physician or a barrister... I always knew that one day I would have my father's estate to look after, so I didn't necessarily *have* to find an occupation, but I was going mad with my inability to do anything."

"So you joined the military."

"I did," he nodded, warmth flooding through him as he

remembered the day he had joined, how proud he was, how much he was looking forward to joining the war effort, to doing something for himself and his country.

"And you loved it," she said, her voice soft, her head tilted at her revelation.

"I suppose you could say that," he said gruffly. "Make no mistake, there were some horrific moments, battles that I wouldn't wish anyone to have to live through, after seeing so many die during them. I have seen injuries as gruesome as they come, men in such pain that they would have rather died. But I finally found my place. Because of my family's position and my own ambition, I rose quickly through the ranks of the army, and by the end, I was helping to plan strategy."

Her eyes were wide as he spoke, and she began to nod. "I can see it," she said. "And it explains why you feel so trapped here at our inn, in our seaside town. You were clearly injured... what brought you here?"

Nathaniel tapped his fingers against his knees. He had been given explicit orders to tell no one of whom he was or what had happened, and there was no one else in the world who could ever have convinced him to do such a thing.

But Daisy... she looked at him with all of her wide-eyed innocence, and he couldn't help but tell her. He explained to her all that had happened — the plot to find Napoleon's future plans, his own success, and how the injury had prevented him from furthering his mission.

"So they sent me here, in order that I might hide out, that all would believe me to be dead. There are spies within the English camp — spies everywhere, to be honest — and so it was the only way to ensure the French were not aware of what we had."

Daisy exhaled slowly, as though she had been holding

her breath the entire time he had been speaking.

"Is Nathaniel Hawke your real name?"

"Nathaniel is," he confirmed.

"I'm glad of it," she said with the slightest of smiles. "I wouldn't have wanted to think that I was calling you by a name not your own since I had met you."

"Not my given name, Daisy," he murmured, "I wouldn't want to hear the name of any other man on your lips."

She bit her rosy bottom lip at that, torturing him, and Nathaniel began to lean in to take that succulent mouth with his. But first, she had one more question, and she raised one hand as if to hold him off.

"How long do you suppose you will remain with us?"

"I honestly do not know," he said with a sigh and a shrug of his shoulders as he moved back again. "But if the last letter was any indication of what is to come, they should be executing the next attack any day now, if they haven't already. So it could be anytime from a day to a week."

She nodded slowly, keeping her gaze down and away from him, and Nathaniel knew exactly what she was thinking — that their time together was too short, that they needed more of it in order to better come to know one another. He wanted to tell her not to fret, that they would be together no matter what was to come, but he couldn't, as of yet, promise that. He hardly knew what would be awaiting him once he returned to London. How could he ask her to leave everything behind to follow him to a life that he wasn't even yet sure of? He would just have to wait, he decided, and determine what the future might hold for them.

But for now, he would enjoy this moment, this time with her. He leaned in once more, softly stroked her face until it was tilted up toward him, and took her lips in a kiss that said more than his words currently could.

14

A titled, wealthy family. Time together that could end at any moment.

It was difficult for Daisy to focus on anything but all that Nathaniel had just told her as they returned to the inn in time for her to prepare that evening's dinner. She was grateful for all he had shared with her, truly she was, but in the same breath, it was difficult to know where they could possibly go from here. Daisy preferred to live her life knowing what was to come, and now it was as though everything she knew to be true had changed.

For there were now two incredibly different possibilities. One was more of a dream than anything — the thought that she could leave here and be with Nathaniel in a world she wouldn't even recognize. It was frightening, and she wasn't sure if it was a future she would welcome. Not only that, she had no inkling as to whether or not Nathaniel had any thought for her in his life beyond his stay here at the inn. Was she simply a way to pass the time, to relieve the boredom that the hole of the military had left within him?

The other path was the familiar, the one to which she

had resigned herself — spending her life managing and maintaining this inn. It hadn't been an altogether unwelcome future for herself — that is, until she had come to know Nathaniel. For the thought of her life to be empty of him once more caused a very unfamiliar ache to begin deep within her. An ache that she certainly hadn't felt when Stephen had left her for Almira.

She wanted to be upset that Nathaniel had, until now, kept from her the fact that he was tied to the nobility, but with all she had said about them, could she blame him? She could see now why his initial attitude had been what it was, but she could only hope that now he better understood the workings of the inn.

Could she ever become used to the idea of someone serving her? The thought caused her to feel slightly sick, for Daisy was used to doing everything in life for herself. But if she and Nathaniel— *no, Daisy, do not get ahead of yourself*, she cautioned. That would only lead to heartache.

Daisy's stomach began to turn as they started up the walk to the inn, for an unfamiliar stately black horse was being led down the road to the stables which were housed next door. Someone was visiting the inn, and, as far as she was aware, they certainly had not been expecting anyone. It might just be a traveler passing through — they had those now and again, though Southwold was not exactly on the path between any major centers. It might also be someone visiting a relative — but then anyone with such a horse could only be tied to the Mansel estate, and they had plenty of rooms to house someone within. No, the most likely possibility was one she did not welcome.

Daisy stole a look at Nathaniel, whose own face had creased as he clearly understood the significance of this guest as well as she now did. Daisy swallowed and closed her eyes. She and Nathaniel had just found one another; had only today, really, come to an understanding about who they were and what the future could hold. Now he would already be going away.

She entered the inn with trepidation, Nathaniel following her, while Daisy's sisters rushed in to greet them.

"Daisy, you will never guess— oh," Iris skidded to a stop on her soft kid slippers as she saw that Daisy wasn't alone. "Mr. Hawke. You, ah, have a visitor."

"A man from the military," Violet added helpfully, and Nathaniel nodded, turning to Daisy, his brown eyes filled with concern as he looked down on her. Despite the fact her sisters were watching, he placed his hands on her arms.

"Thank you for the lovely picnic lunch, Daisy," he said while smiling down at her. "All will be fine."

Daisy nodded mutely, unsure of how to respond to his words. She wanted to agree with him, but then she knew that to believe his words could be more than she could bear if they proved false. Nathaniel didn't even know for what this man had come, so how could he tell her that all would be fine? The man could send him back to the front lines, only for him to be killed. How could *that* be fine?

She knew she was being dramatic, but she couldn't help herself. As Nathaniel continued into her father's study, where apparently the man awaited, Daisy swallowed hard and looked at her sisters, who stared back at her without a word. They had spent most of the day teasing her about the time she was spending with the man she had initially disdained but Daisy had shrugged it off, at least until she knew more about what could ever happen between the two of them. She was being overly cautious, not wanting to repeat the situation with Stephen, yet she had never felt anything close to Stephen as what she did for Nathaniel.

But now that she knew more about him, understood the possibility of him leaving... she turned and fled up to her bedroom, where she would compose herself for whatever news Nathaniel would provide.

~

NATHANIEL ENTERED THE DARK STUDY, allowing a moment for his eyes to adjust within the room that offered little daylight through the small corner window covered by a curtain. He supposed that Tavners enjoyed napping in here more than anything else, but he couldn't fault the man who was jovial enough as he left the study where he had been hosting General Collins to leave the two of them alone.

"You say you were a friend of his?" Nathaniel asked, as he took the seat Tavners had vacated, and Collins laughed.

"At one time, we were as close as could be. The man has certainly settled into this life here at the inn, but whether or not you can believe it, he was a competent soldier and I owe him my life as I would have been killed had he not seen the man approaching me from behind in battle. But that's a story for another day." The general leaned back in his chair, assessing Nathaniel. "I must say, life by the sea looks good on you."

Nathaniel chuckled. He wasn't sure what to say — that no, it wasn't the seaside life but a woman, the daughter of the man who had taken him in, who had brought about the change within him?

"There are... certain aspects of my stay that I have enjoyed," he finally said, and the general raised an eyebrow, as though he understood much from Nathaniel's few words.

"I'm glad to hear it," was all he said. "And I have news for you — good news. The plan worked. We were able to ambush the French troops with a complete surprise attack. I wouldn't say the war is won, but we certainly sent them retreating. A good day for England, Major-General, a very good day. All thanks to your strategy and bravery. Which is why I came myself to tell you of it. I had to return to England for a time anyway, and didn't see why I couldn't make one quick stop in Southwold."

Nathaniel grinned, unable to hide the pleasure he felt at the words, knowing that he had helped bring about such a victory.

"I'm more than glad to hear it, General," he said. "I would have given anything to be there, of course, to be part of the attack, but the fact that the plan worked... well, it's all one could ask for, really."

"And now, even better news," the general continued. "You no longer must play the role of a dead man. I have already sent a letter informing your family that you do, in fact, live, and will be returning home with an injury. We had not informed them of your supposed death, so hopefully, no word was brought back to them that would have caused any distress. You can now return home, and assume the title and role that is waiting for you, *your grace*."

The address, attributed to him, still seemed foreign, making Nathaniel want to turn and look about for anyone else in the room to whom the general might be speaking.

"I still can hardly believe it — the Duke of Greenwich," Nathaniel said, shaking his head, and the general grinned.

"Believe it. Tavners has arranged for you to hire a horse from the stables nearby for your return to London if you're up for riding. I am headed that way myself, and I believe we could make the trip in three days if we stop every few hours. Or I could arrange for a carriage to be sent to pick you up."

"I'll ride," Nathaniel said immediately, in hopes the

general would see that he was fit — for riding or any role the military might offer him. But, alas, a duke was not sent to the battlefield.

"Very well," the general said. "I shall stay the night and we will be off in the morning."

In the morning. And then he would be returning to London, to a new life. It only gave him a few hours to decide what exactly he could — or should — say to Daisy before he departed. He needed to explain all to her, to ask her to wait for him to return. He would settle into whatever life might hold, and then he would determine what to do and come to tell her of it. Only, of what promise he could make to her, he had no idea.

15

Nathaniel and the general had been ensconced in her father's study for some time now. Daisy couldn't sit and wait any longer, and so she had started downstairs, beginning to prepare for the dinner to come. She had to keep herself busy — it was the only way she knew how to cope.

She was in the midst of mashing potatoes when Iris came flying into the room, Marigold behind her.

"Daisy!" Iris exclaimed. "I *must* tell you what I've learned! You will never believe it."

"Iris," Marigold scolded, out of breath from chasing after her sister. "I told you to not say anything. Give the man a chance to tell her himself."

"What is it?" Daisy asked, her heart beating fast as she turned to look at the two of them. Iris was simply bursting with her news, while Marigold glared at her sister disapprovingly. Obviously, Iris had been listening at the keyhole again. It irked the lot of them that there was never a private conversation to be had in this house, but then, that was life with Iris. Tonight it might apparently prove to be a blessing for Daisy.

"Iris..." Marigold threatened, but Iris was not to be prevented — and Daisy needed to know what it was that had her in such a frenzy.

"Tell me," she demanded.

"Mr. Hawke is a *duke*!" Iris practically crowed.

Daisy dropped the spoon she was holding onto the floor, hearing it clatter, though it seemed as though the sound was coming from elsewhere, that she was removed from her body and watching from a distance.

"Not only is he a duke," Iris continued in both awe and excitement, "But he was a major-general in the army, and he is returning to London — tomorrow — to assume his new role under the title of a duke. A title that came to him while he was at war. Can you believe it?"

Daisy stood in shock, hardly able to process the information.

"B-but he said his family was wealthy, and connected to the nobility— he never said anything about a title, let alone him a... duke. He told me his father held no title whatsoever!"

Daisy dimly noted Marigold walking over and taking her elbow, leading her over to one of the chairs in the corner of the kitchen.

"Maybe he just hasn't had a chance to tell you yet," Marigold said reassuringly, and Daisy noted Violet nodding — she must have followed her two sisters into the kitchen.

"He had every chance," Daisy said, her tone flat. "He chose not to. He clearly saw no reason for me to know."

"Daisy..." Violet said, ever the romantic, though she clearly didn't know what to say at the moment.

"It's fine," Daisy said, attempting to push the hurt aside

as she stood to return to her duties. "It was nothing but a flirtation. There was no reason for him to tell me, as following his departure — tomorrow — it won't matter at all."

"Are you sure about that?" Marigold asked gently. "I know you haven't spoken much of it to us, but it seems as though you've become close to Mr. Hawke in a short time."

Daisy shook her head. "It matters not at all. He has proven to be the same man I thought him to be upon his arrival here."

She picked up her masher and returned to the stove, though this time she had renewed vigor as she attacked the potatoes.

She had been a fool, allowing herself to raise her hopes for a man who saw her as nothing but a dalliance, a way to pass the time as he awaited his return to his former life. How stupid she would have seemed to him — the daughter of an innkeeper, who spent her days in the marketplace and the kitchen, actually believing that she might have a future with him — a duke! Thank goodness she hadn't said anything to him of it, that they had shared nothing more than a couple of kisses. Kisses that, to her, had meant everything, had seemed as though they held so much emotion within them, more than their words ever had. To him, she was just another woman, just another kiss.

Typical.

Daisy felt the tears pricking at the back of her eyes, the burn in her throat as she fought back the tears. Tears of anger, she told herself — not hurt. She couldn't allow a man like him to hurt her. Why was it that anytime a good-looking man of some worth came her way she thought herself deserving enough to be more to him than a passing thought? Well, no more. She was done. Done with men, done with believing that there might be more for her in life than this inn.

"Daisy..." It was Iris now, which meant that Daisy must truly be allowing her emotions to show, if Iris should be attempting to comfort her. "I'm sorry, I shouldn't have—"

"It's fine, Iris."

"I didn't know... didn't think that he meant—"

"He means nothing. Now, are the lot of you going to help me or just stand there deciding whether or not I've been well and truly jilted once more?"

Her sisters silently donned their aprons, washed their hands, and began to chop vegetables and prepare the meal alongside her. Knowing Daisy as well as they did, they said nothing more but offered their support with their silent presence. They might bicker and tease one another often enough, but when it mattered... they were there.

NATHANIEL WAS surprised when Daisy's three sisters served them supper, but she was nowhere to be seen. He asked the redhead, Marigold, where she was, but the girl simply shrugged and looked at him as though he had offended her. He had no idea what he might have said to insult her so, but worry ate at him for the rest of the meal. Something was obviously amiss — was it the general's presence? Daisy was a smart woman and would have known what it meant that he was here. She was upset, and he understood that — but why was she avoiding him?

Of the three sisters serving, the youngest, Violet, thin with a whimsical expression continually on her face, seemed to be looking at him with the most sympathy. When he and the general rose to leave the table, he tapped her on the shoulder just as she began to walk toward the entrance to the kitchen.

"Will you ask Daisy to meet me?" he asked quietly, and when she bit her lip, seemingly unsure, he added, "Please?"

She must have heard the desperation in his tone, for she sighed and relented.

"Fine," she said. "Go down to the shore beyond the back of the inn in a couple of hours. I cannot promise she will be there, but I will ask her."

Nathaniel nodded. "Thank you, Miss Tavners."

Violet hesitantly smiled, nodded her head, and then when her older sisters began to glare at her from the kitchen door, hurried in after them.

Nathaniel could feel the general's stare on him as he left the room, but decided, so be it. He had to talk to Daisy, to tell her that this was not goodbye… but that he would talk to her again soon.

Two hours later, he found himself standing in the sand beyond the inn, staring at the sea with the wind whipping his hair across the back of his neck. He had been here for some time — far past when he and Violet had agreed — and still, Daisy had not arrived.

He'd wait a few more minutes, he decided. Then he would return to the inn and do whatever it took to find her, even if that meant searching out her bedchamber in the family's private quarters. He and the general were to leave at first light, and he couldn't do so without saying goodbye to her — or, if she would allow it, goodbye for now.

Just as he was about to turn to leave, a soft tap on his shoulder caused him to whirl around. There she was, the sound of her footsteps having been masked by the waves and the soft sand.

She had approached like a spirit, and she nearly looked like one as well. Her dark hair, normally so tight against her head, was unbound around her shoulders, her light blue dress billowing around her legs in the wind, pressing the material tight against her bodice. She was breathtakingly beautiful, and suddenly all Nathaniel wanted to do was throw himself at her feet and ask her to be his, forever.

But that wouldn't be fair. To him or to her, nor to the responsibility that awaited him.

"Daisy," he breathed as she stood there, staring at him as motionless as a statue. "I was afraid that you wouldn't come."

"It is your last night, is it not?" she said, just loud enough for him to hear over the wind and the waves. "Were you hoping to end your time with me here on a high note? Take me on the beach, is that it?"

He nearly recoiled at her words, struck toward him like a sword through the air.

"Of course not," he said, upset that she would think such a thing of him. "Is that why you are upset? You believe that I was only toying with you during my stay here? Listen, Daisy—"

He reached a hand out to her, but she took a step backward, and he took a breath and continued.

"I am leaving tomorrow, it is true. I attempted to tell you the moment I knew myself, but you were nowhere to be found. The attack was successful, and I am now able to resume my life and return home."

"I am happy for you," she said quickly, though her tone conveyed certain displeasure.

"I will be honest," he said, and she quirked an eyebrow

upwards. "When I came here I, of course, had no idea that I would fall for a woman, particularly the daughter of the innkeeper, the man who was providing me a safe haven. But there is something between us that I cannot deny. I will return to London with the general tomorrow, determine that all of my affairs are in order, and then I will come back to Southwold to see you once more."

He heard the words in his ears, knew they sounded trite and lacked any sort of promise besides a visit, but he couldn't commit to her — not until he fully understood what was waiting for him upon his return.

"What affairs?" she asked, holding his gaze, and he cleared his throat.

"I'm not sure what you mean?"

"What must you place in order?" she asked, the words emerging slowly, as though he wouldn't otherwise understand her. "Are you not the son of an untitled though wealthy man, with no career to return to?"

He should tell her, he knew he should, and yet, he was worried that if he did, it would be the last she would ever speak to him. It would be different once he could explain what becoming a duke would be like, how it would change the life that he would soon be assuming. At the moment, however, he had no idea himself, so how was he ever supposed to broach the subject with her?

"That is true," he said, and for the most part, it was. "But I have not been in England in quite some time, so I must sort out my living arrangements."

She nodded.

"Well, if that is all, Nathaniel, then I wish you the best of luck in your travels. But rest assured, there is no need to return. I have enjoyed this flirtation as much as you have and have no need to be reminded of it in the future."

"But Daisy..." he managed, shock filling him at her words. Had he misread the situation? He had thought there was more growing between them, but if this was what she truly thought...

She turned to leave, and Nathaniel reached forward, curling his fingers around her arm.

"Daisy," he repeated, more firmly this time. "Do you truly believe that our relationship was only a flirtation? Because to me, it was far more than that."

She lifted her eyes to him, the blue-green of them as stormy as the sea beyond where they stood.

"Truly?" she asked. "And just where would I fit in the life of a duke?"

Her question stunned him. How did she know? When had she found out?

"I... I'm not entirely sure," he said, not denying her words. "That is what I need to determine."

"So you are a duke, then?"

"I suppose I am," he said slowly. "I have only just recently learned the news. My grandfather was the Duke of Greenwich. The title passed to his son, my uncle. Days before I arrived here, the general told me that both my uncle and my cousin, the heir to the title, died from an illness that swept through their village. Which leaves it with me. I would have told you, Daisy, truly I would have, but I have no idea what to expect once I return to London. Once I learn more and have a better understanding of the life I will lead, then I will return to you, I promise."

"Once you determine if I would fit in a life such as the one you would lead, you mean?" she asked, and now the anger seemed to have dissipated, though Nathaniel thought he would have far preferred it to the distress that remained.

"I am truly sorry about your relatives, Nathaniel. But still, you lied to me."

"I only ask that you give me some time to come to terms with what my life is now going to be like," he pleaded, but she shook her head.

"You will return, you will find that women are altogether quite interested in a handsome duke, and you will forget about the daughter of an innkeeper in a little seaside town."

Her eyes were filling with tears, but Nathaniel worried that if he reached out to her once more, she would only push him away again.

"Wait for me, Daisy."

"Wait for you? To return for a visit?" She shook her head, blinking away tears, breaking his heart.

"It's far better that we go our separate ways now, Nathaniel, before this becomes anything more than what it is. I wish you all the best as you enter your new life. Goodbye, Nathaniel. Your grace."

She turned on her heel and walked away, back through the sand. Nathaniel longed to run after her, to take her in his arms and kiss her senseless, but then what would he say? For she was right in that he didn't have an answer for her — not right now. He would just have to continue on as he planned, and hope that she would wait for him.

16

Daisy stopped in shock when she walked into the room, unable to believe the sight that awaited her.

It had been over two weeks now since the day Nathaniel — that is, the Duke of Greenwich — had ridden away from The Wild Rose Inn, back to London to assume a life of privilege. She had watched him from the upper window of her bedroom, allowing only one tear to emerge as he rode away, out of her life forever.

What a little fool she had been, thinking that, perhaps, this man would want her — *her*, Daisy Tavners, daughter of an innkeeper. She had hoped, when she had gone to him that night on the beach, that he had wanted to see her in order to tell her of who he truly was, to tell her of what he was returning home to. But no, he had continued on with his charade, telling her enough of the truth so that she would believe him but not enough to be completely convincing.

For whatever reason, she was simply a woman with

whom men entertained themselves until their true selves were revealed and they found another direction.

He had asked her to wait, but for what? To become his mistress? For she knew, with all certainty, that he would never take her as his wife. Stephen had certainly been clear in his explanation to her that a baron certainly could never take a common woman from the village to wed. So how, then, could a duke ever do so? Nathaniel thought with one word, one command, she would do as he said, but he should know by now that would never work.

She had thought all was fine and that everyone had continued on in the lives they were meant to live. So why now, when she walked into the family sitting room, were her three sisters and Millie sitting there in wait for her, staring at her as though she had made the biggest mistake of her life?

"What is it?" she asked, standing there looking down upon them.

"We simply wanted to talk to you," Marigold said. "Sit, please?"

Daisy rolled her eyes and sighed, but took a seat. If there were any people in the world she would agree to listen to, it was the four women in front of her. But whatever could it be about?"

"Daisy," Millie began, looking to the rest of them, who nodded at her. "We know that Mr. Hawke's departure has been rather difficult for you."

"I believe he is Nathaniel Huntingwell, Duke of Greenwich," Daisy corrected, but without malice — it was not Millie's fault the man was not who he had claimed to be.

"Yes, well, perhaps we should simply call him Nathaniel within this room," Millie said, continuing. "You have been so despondent since he left. It leads us to believe that perhaps you felt more toward him than you claim. He told you that he would come back. Perhaps you should write a letter to him, or keep the idea of being with him open."

"Why would I do such a thing?" Daisy asked, surprised that her friend would even suggest it.

"Oh, Daisy, it's only that, having recently found love myself, I do know how wonderful it can be, and I have such a wish for the same to happen to you. I saw you with him, Daisy, and the way you looked at him, and he at you... no one could deny that you felt something for one another."

"At first I felt nothing but frustration," Daisy said, the slightest of smiles threatening to tease her lips as she thought of just how they had clashed upon first meeting. "It should have stayed that way."

"But the way he looked at you..." Violet chimed in, her expression wistful, and Daisy was already shaking her head.

"I do not deny that there was something between us, but it was nothing that would last beyond his time here," Daisy said firmly. "I thank you all, and I know you only have my best interests and happiness at heart, but please, please do not push this any further. I am done with thinking of Nathaniel, and I wish you wouldn't suggest that I do otherwise."

She gave them each a pointed stare, and they reluctantly nodded.

Daisy knew how much they loved her, as she did each of them in turn. But as she left the room, needing another moment alone — and this would be the last tear she shed for this man, she promised herself — she could hear their murmurings, which made her feel ill. She was supposed to be the one to look after them, not the other way around. She didn't like the feeling of being the one the others worried about, for her role had always been to look after them, fussing around the lot of them. She would just have to convince them that she was perfectly fine, she determined. Then they could all leave her be.

Daisy had been right about one thing, Nathaniel mused as he sat at what was now his desk, in what was now his study, awake for another sleepless night as he attempted to sort through the mess of documents his uncle had left him. He supposed that the man had known what he was about, but Nathaniel was perplexed by the way he had kept all of his ledgers, the disorganized state of the lot of them. He figured his cousin had been shown it all, but his cousin was no longer with them, and so the knowledge of the Dukedom of Greenwich was contained in the papers within this office, those of the country estates, and within the minds of the stewards who had served his uncle.

He sighed, sitting back and running his hands through his hair, which was far too long. If there was one positive out of all of this, it was the fact that he could see himself enjoying this role, once he made sense of it all. He was provided with a sense of power, over his own properties and estates, as well as influencing others around him. He could exert his influence in multiple facets, and he wouldn't be shy about doing so, particularly in the arena of military affairs.

What Daisy had been right about? The fact that he certainly didn't lack for women interested in him anymore. While it was not as though he never received any attention from mothers and daughters of the upper class, now he could hardly walk into a room or take a step down a Mayfair street without an introduction to yet another young lady. They were lovely, truly they were, but none had his heart beating in an unusual pattern as had Daisy Tavners.

If he were being honest, she had left his thoughts for nary a moment since he had ridden away from the inn two weeks ago. As he had left, he couldn't shake the feeling that he was leaving something — someone — behind. And now... he had no idea what to do. For her parting words to him had basically said that she saw him as nothing but a dalliance for a brief interlude. He was well aware that she hadn't even liked him at first. Maybe knowing who he was, that he had kept the truth from her, was enough to break whatever tie had begun to form between them.

The more time he spent within this home, however, the more he recognized just how barren it was. The London manor was particularly large, which only added to the feeling of hollowness as there was only himself and the servants to fill it. His aunt lived with him when she was in London but was choosing to spend most of her time in the dower house of the Chelmsford estate. She said it was where she felt comfortable, where she best remembered her family, and besides that, her daughter had married a nobleman with a nearby estate, and now with a grandchild on the way, she desired to be close to them.

Leaving Nathaniel alone.

He had always thought that he was happy that way. Before he left for war, he had taken rooms in a boarding-house to provide himself the independence he had been searching for. But now... when he looked around the rooms, he was finding himself imagining what Daisy would choose to do with them. When he sat down to dinner, he wondered what Daisy would have chosen for the menu. And when he went to bed at night, he pictured her there, lying beside him, her head on the pillow with her dark hair splayed around it, unbound as it had been the last night on the shore.

This house might be one of awe and splendor, but in a strong sense, it lacked what was most important, what he had felt at the inn. It was devoid of people, devoid of love. When he had stayed at The Wild Rose Inn, at the time he had focused on all of its shortcomings, but there was one thing he could always count on, and that was the presence of another person, whether it be one of the Johnsons or the Tavners themselves. While everyone had their faults, no one had been anything but welcoming to him, and he missed that.

He wondered what Daisy was doing right now. Was she sitting with her family? Or in her bedroom, looking out that window over the street? Or was she walking along the shoreline — alone?

Where did he wish she was? Sitting beside him, helping figure out the mess in front of him. For some reason, he knew without question she would be able to do so. She seemed to have the ability to do whatever she put her mind to.

Nathaniel looked up from his desk to the portrait of his uncle staring at him from across the room. He had been a good man. Absent-minded, but he loved his family and he did his best at maintaining his responsibilities. He would never have imagined that his nephew would be the one assuming his role.

Nathaniel shook his head, allowing himself the smallest of chuckles.

And then, he knew. Nathaniel would never be able to put his finger on why, in that particular moment, the revelation had come to him, but come to him it had.

It didn't matter what his responsibilities were. They were

numerous to be sure, but they were not insurmountable. It didn't matter what the expectations were on his wife. No one had expected him to be here in this role, yet here he was. So why could his wife not be who she damn well pleased? It should matter to no one but himself.

All that mattered was that he found a woman who was perfect for him. And he had done so — within an inn in a little seaside village called Southwold.

He loved Daisy Tavners. He had not known her long, but everything he knew about her to be true spoke to his heart and his soul, and he missed her with a ferocity he had never known before. He missed her more than the war, more than the strategic plans he had made, more than the perfect functioning of his left leg.

Nathaniel needed her in his life, and he knew suddenly that he must go to whatever lengths necessary in order for her to understand how he felt. He could only hope that she truly, deep inside, felt the same for him.

Despite the late hour, he began to make preparations. He would leave the very next day. While his leg was not yet completely healed — not that it ever would be whole, according to the few physicians he had spoken with — he could still ride, but his journey would be slightly longer than that of an able-bodied man. And so, unable to wait any longer, he scribbled a hasty note, lit the wax, sealed the letter, and placed it where he knew his butler would find it to post early the very next day.

He hoped it was enough to melt her heart, just enough that he could convince her to allow it to fuse with his.

17

Daisy stared at the note in her hand.

It was short, succinct, and completely confusing.

Wait for me, Daisy — please? All my love, Nathaniel.

They were the very words he had last spoken to her on the shore behind the inn. To wait for him. She had questioned what she was waiting for, had denied that she could mean anything to him but a potential woman to bed.

She re-read the words again. They were the same words with an exception — he had added the "please" — and a question mark. It was what had been missing — the question, as opposed to an order.

Then there were the closing words. "All my love." Did he mean them? Did he — *could* he — actually love her? She didn't think she had given him much reason to. But why else would he sign it in such a fashion?

Daisy didn't want to provide herself that hope once more, but she couldn't deny that the words caused warmth unlike anything she had ever felt before to course through her. For the truth of it was, she loved him, sincerely, with all of her heart. She had tried to deny it for so long, but as she read the note in front of her over and over again, she couldn't help the tears from coursing down her cheeks anew. This time, however, they were tears of another sort — not tears of sorrow, but of partial relief over her acceptance of the fact and hope that, despite her best intentions, was now invading its way back into her soul.

But Daisy was not the type of woman to wait. She was not going to sit around until he determined it was time to come back for her. If he wanted her, he was going to have to accept that she was his, now or never, and no matter what the future held for them. For if he did love her, as she did him, then she knew there was nothing they couldn't do together.

Daisy looked up now at the mantel clock in her family's sitting room. It was two in the afternoon, which would provide her no time to leave today. She would prepare in the next few hours and leave on the morrow — though first, she had to speak with Marigold and ensure all was well in hand.

Marigold, it turned out, was more than accepting of Daisy's intentions. She did look a little panicked at the mention of managing most of the work of the inn — overseeing the meals, going to market each day, and the process of preparing for new guests — but she nodded determinately at all Daisy said. Finally, however, she did find a quill pen and paper and began to make notes.

They were in the midst of this process when their father entered the sitting room, wondering just when did Daisy think she was going out to the marketplace?

"It's a slow day, Father," she said, hardly looking up at him. "Now that the Johnsons have returned to the farmyard, we have no guests."

"Dinner must still be prepared for the family," he said.

"And never fear, we have a new influx of guests arriving next week."

He looked pleased as he said it, and Daisy couldn't help raising an eyebrow to him.

"Men from the war effort, perhaps?" she asked dryly, but all he did was shrug his shoulders.

Apparently, his first experiment, in Nathaniel's stay, had been considered a success.

"I have to speak to you of something, Father," she said, her chin set and her words emerging just as her mother walked in behind him. "I must be going — at least for a time."

"Go?" her mother exclaimed. "To the market?"

"No, Mama. I must go to London."

"To London!" her mother and father shouted simultaneously.

"You cannot!" her father determined.

"What will we do?" her mother added, her hands in front of her chest, pleading.

Daisy took a deep breath.

"You will manage," she said, realizing that she actually believed it. She had thought that she had to keep everything under her own tight control, but Nathaniel was right — her family had been fine before she looked after things, and they would be able to do so again. "Marigold is more than prepared to go to the marketplace and oversee the preparation of the meals. And Mother, Father, you managed this inn long before I was ever old enough to take any responsibility. I'm sure you will be able to do so again in my absence."

"How long will you be gone for?" her mother asked, tears coming to her eyes.

"I'm not sure," Daisy replied. She could be gone a week,

she could be gone forever — she had no idea. It all depended upon Nathaniel.

"And you cannot go *alone*," her mother continued, her hands waving wildly in the air now as she began to pace around the room.

"I shall be fine, Mother," Daisy said, attempting to calm her. "I will take the stagecoach to London. It will take a few days, but it is perfectly respectable. I will write to you when I arrive."

"I'm not sure..."

"There is no one else who can leave to accompany me."

Her parents looked at one another, as though they were aware that they should not allow her to travel alone, yet clearly, neither of them wanted to accompany her, nor did they want to spare another who might be needed at the inn.

"When would you leave?" her father asked.

"Tomorrow morning," Daisy said, her chin set determinately, and seeing her expression, knowing it well, her father nodded.

"Very well," he said before showing that he observed far more than he allowed his daughters to see. "Let's hope the duke will accept you. If not, you will always have a home here with us."

DAISY'S EYES were watering the next morning as she hugged her family farewell. They might not always seem to be the closest of families, but when it mattered, they were there for one another no matter what threatened. It would be the first circumstance in which they would be truly separated for a long period of time, and Daisy wished her mother would stop crying, for she was now tearing up herself.

"I will write immediately upon arriving, and perhaps I will be home much sooner than you think," Daisy said with a teary smile of her own. "Best of luck, and love to you all!" She walked down the road to the middle of the village and the post office, where the stagecoach was to arrive. There, she was told that she likely had another hour or so, and Daisy sighed in frustration. Having no wish to wait around the post office, attempting to answer questions of other villagers regarding just why she was going to London, and not wanting to return home to repeat their tearful goodbyes, she decided that she had time for a quick foray to the meadow — her meadow, which was but a few minutes' walk out of Southwold.

The postmaster confirmed that she could leave her valise with him and all would be quite safe, and Daisy took off at a quick pace. She would collect a few blooms of bluebells to take with her, to remind her of the scent of her treasured field, for there was no other way to quite capture the scent of the flower.

Daisy thought she could likely find the path to her meadow with her eyes closed, and close them she did once she reached it. As she stood still beside her tree, she breathed in the scent around her which, no matter where she went, would always speak to her of home.

The warmth of the sun's rays fell upon her face, and she finally opened her eyes in order to see it. She was about to take a step forward but gasped in surprise at the sight before her. Her heart slowed to a stop, her limbs remained immobile, and all she could do was stand and stare.

Never before had she seen anything that had so stunned her. Daisy watched mutely as the man in front of her slowed his horse to a stop before gingerly dismounting, his face distorted in some pain.

But he made no other show of it as he knelt, gathered a handful of bluebells, and brought them to his nose before carefully tucking them into the saddlebag, which was already full near to bursting.

Daisy couldn't believe her eyes, that he was here, not only in Southwold but in her meadow. It was as though she were barely breathing, but she must have made some form of movement, for suddenly his head snapped up, his body moving into a position of readiness for battle. He cringed as the sudden weight upon his leg must have bothered him, but he remained in position as though he were bracing for an attack, as though he were still at war.

Daisy finally took a step forward, out of the shadows and into the sunlight, and called out to him from across the meadow.

"Nathaniel," she cried, hearing her own voice hesitant and yet... desperate. These were not emotions she enjoyed experiencing, but when it came to him, it seemed she had no control.

His head snapped up and around, his gaze finding her, and then without a thought, she picked up her skirts and ran toward him as he dropped the lead of his horse and did the same toward her. She remained silent as tears fell down her cheeks the closer he came, until suddenly the length of meadow that was between them fell away, and she was in his arms, which lifted her up off the ground, swinging her around as she clung to him in equal measure. She had no idea how he didn't fall to the ground upon his leg, but apparently, his right was strong enough to hold them both up. The moment he set her back on the ground, ever so gently allowing her feet to touch, his lips descended upon hers, roving over them in a passionate fire that would have caused her to weep were she not already crying.

His strong hands wrapped around her head, kneading into her scalp, loosening her chignon. Her arms were so tight around his neck she thought she might be choking him, but when she loosened them even the slightest, he simply held her closer, as though he didn't want to bear the thought of her ever letting go.

Their lips found one another once more, their mouths fused together, pouring out the love they felt for each other, until finally, finally, he took a step back from her, his breath coming as rapidly and harshly as her own.

"You came back," she said, her voice just above a whisper.

"I told you I would," he said, cupping her face with his hands, his soft thumbs stroking her cheeks over and over, wiping away her tears.

"I'm so sorry," she choked out. "I should have trusted you, should have known that—"

He held up one hand between them in order to stop her flow of words.

"You have nothing to apologize for. It was me who should have been honest with you from the start."

"I understand."

"Daisy," he insisted, his brown eyes darkening as he looked down on her. "I love you. I believe I have loved you from the day we ran into one another, you with your bag from the market. You are practical, you see things through, and yet you do it all in a manner so loving, for I know you take it all on in order to allow others in your life the freedom to do as they please, be what they wish to be. I was a fool to question how you might fit into my life, for the truth is, Daisy, it is no life without you in it. I realize that now, and I can only hope it is not too late."

He knelt down within the bluebells in front of her, and

Daisy gasped. His handsome face looked up at her, pleading, as he took her hands within his.

"Daisy Tavners," Nathaniel said, his voice just above a murmur. "I love you with all that I am and I long for you to be my wife. See me not as Nathaniel Huntingwell, Duke of Greenwich, but as the man you came to know over my time here. If you feel anything akin to the same for me, I beg of you... consider my words, consider my offer, consider... me. Be my wife, Daisy, please. Say yes."

Daisy's lips curled up into a smile. She was still in shock as she could hardly believe that this man, this duke, could want her, Daisy Tavners. But here he was, asking for her hand in marriage in the middle of her meadow with a sincerity in his eyes that spoke of nothing but love.

"Of course I will say yes," she said, and he let out a loud whoop and stood, twirling her around in the air once more.

"Stop!" she said, laughing. "Your leg!"

"I can hardly feel it," he said, "Knowing that you have agreed to be with me — for the rest of our lives — seems to have miraculously healed me."

She laughed at the ridiculousness of his words as he set her back down and brought his hands to her arms.

"I must tell you though, Daisy," he said, his brow furrowing slightly, "Life will change, as I'm sure you are well aware. The life of a duchess may sound glamorous to most, but it will be work, most of all becoming immune to some of the barbed manners of the *ton*. But there are good people among them too, Daisy, and I can hardly wait to see how you will turn around the entirety of my estate, for I know that if there is anyone who can do it — it is you."

"You are not marrying me simply for my skills in managing your estates, are you?" she teased.

But instead of laughing, he turned serious, his eyes dark

as he hovered over her once more. "Never," he breathed. "I want you for the woman you are and the man you help me become."

Daisy had never heard anything more beautiful, and she threw herself back into his arms to show him just how much they meant to her.

18

The weight Nathaniel had been carrying since he'd left the military and taken on his ducal responsibilities lifted when Daisy said yes to his proposal. He had had plenty of time to think as he had traveled here alone, and far too many times when he ran the scenario through his head, it had ended with her denying him.

That she had said yes, without hesitation… he could hardly believe it.

"I was on my way to the inn to find you," he said, still incredulous. "I was here to collect you a bouquet — one I thought you would appreciate."

He led her over to his horse, pulling out the bunch of bluebells. He gave them to her, though he felt rather idiotic about it, as they were standing in a field amongst the beautiful blue-violet flower. Daisy, however, didn't seem to mind.

"They are absolutely perfect," she said, holding them to her nose and deeply inhaling. "Thank you."

"Did you ride?" he asked.

"I walked," she said, tilting her head. "Actually… I found out I had some time as I was waiting for the coach."

"The coach?" he asked, confused. "Where were you going?"

"London," she said, a shy smile crossing her face. "I received your letter, and one thing you must know, Nathaniel, is that I do not enjoy waiting. So I was coming to see you myself."

He laughed then, hardly believing that he had almost missed her — had she not come to this meadow, she likely would have already been on the next coach by the time he arrived, their paths missing by just a few moments.

Fortunately, there was a greater power, one which had been hard at work ensuring that their journeys would intersect here, in this place that held so much meaning for the both of them now.

"I shall have to plant you fields of these flowers," he mused, "I promise to do so as a wedding gift to you."

"We shall be able to come to visit, will we not?" Daisy asked suddenly, turning anxious eyes upon him. "To visit my family, and this meadow, and the sea?"

"I shall build you a fine home somewhere near this land if that is what you so wish," he said, but she was already shaking her head.

"Of course not," she scolded him. "Nothing lavish simply because you are a duke. Visits to the Wild Rose Inn will suffice. I understand that life will change once I become a duchess — my word, I can hardly believe I am saying such a thing — but one thing you must know, Nathaniel, is that I have no plans on changing myself."

"Nor would I ever want you to," he assured her. "Though you may have to become used to wearing the odd silk."

She laughed then, a merry, tinkling sound that reached into his heart, wrapping around it and pulling him close to her. He took her in his arms once more, kissing her soundly.

When her tongue crept in to lick at him, he nearly had to step back at the shock that coursed through him from that one tiny movement.

"We best stop," he said, hearing the roughness of his voice, but she shook her head and refused to let go. He cursed inwardly as he found he couldn't deny her, as much as he knew that he should.

He could feel the moment she released the passion within her, and he couldn't help but respond in kind. He wasn't sure how it happened, but one moment they were standing in each other's arms, and the next he was lying back in the field of bluebells, feeling the rich earth beneath him and the sun on his face as his senses were filled with the beauty of the meadow — and the woman above him.

Nathaniel ran his hands down her arms, over her back, and then they were rolling to lie side by side, one of her hands over the stubble on his cheeks, the other within his hair, smoothing it back away from his face.

"I love you," she whispered.

"And I you," he returned.

Her hands slipped within the folds of his linen shirt, and he sat up in order to remove his jacket to lay it beneath them so that she wouldn't dirty her dress. When he lay back down next to her, he couldn't help but run his hands down her bodice, cupping the breasts he had been yearning to touch for weeks now through her thin muslin dress.

She arched into him, helping him slip the fabric from her shoulders to provide him full access, and he murmured her name in delight, hardly believing that she could be so perfect as this.

Daisy's hands came to the fall of his breeches, and he shook his head, but then she pulled back from him, looking him deeply in the eyes, hers stormy once more.

"Make love to me?" she asked, biting her lip, nearly undoing him. "Please — here, in this meadow that has been everything to me as I have waited for you to enter my life, that has become the place where we found one another and the love that we share?"

Nathaniel stopped thinking then, as his body and soul found the woman for whom he had been waiting so long. This time, he permitted her to undo his breeches, while he tenderly lifted her skirts. He held onto all the restraint he had within him as he ran his hands up her smooth legs to find her, ensuring she was ready for him. When she finally nodded, pressing against him with encouraging murmurs, he slowly, carefully entered her. He heard her gasp in his ear as he held her tightly to him, but with tender kisses and caresses, she was soon asking for more.

It began as a soft, slow awakening, ending in an explosion of passion — nearly the opposite of how they had come together. One thing was for certain. Life with Daisy would be a life of satisfaction, one that would challenge him in all the ways he would welcome.

They lay there for a time, smiling at one another in contented bliss, until she finally whispered, "I think I've missed my coach."

He laughed as they helped one another rise, straightened their clothing, and walked to his horse.

"Ride with me?" he asked, and she nodded.

"Always."

Daisy began laughing as they neared her home after collecting her valise, and he asked whatever could be so amusing.

"My family," she said, and he finally saw them all, congregating at the door as they watched their arrival with wide eyes. "I told them I might be home sooner rather than later — as it turns out, I was correct, but in an entirely different way from anything I could have ever imagined."

He joined in her laughter as the two of them dismounted and approached the door.

"Daisy!" Iris exclaimed. "What happened?"

"It seems I had no need to travel to London," she said, turning her face up to Nathaniel. "For what I needed in London came to me."

"Mr. Tavners," Nathaniel said, stepping forward. "I realize I should have come to you first. Please forgive me for not doing so. I would like to ask, however, for permission to marry your daughter — as soon as possible."

Tavners' brows lifted so high they were near to his hairline as he stared at Daisy incredulously, as though he could hardly believe that his eldest daughter might actually not only leave home but marry this man and become a duchess. Nathaniel wondered how much of it was a surprise to him, and of how aware he had been of the possibility.

"This will make you happy, Daisy?" Tavners asked, addressing his daughter, and she nodded with a wide grin on her face.

"Very."

"Then, of course," he said, his lips stretching into a smile as his wife began to squeal beside him. "Welcome to the family, Greenwich. I could use another man within it."

They all laughed then, before Tavners sobered for a moment.

"There is something I must ask, however," to which Nathaniel nodded. "You will return to visit? I can hardly imagine not seeing my daughter for a great length of time."

"Of course," Nathaniel promised. "The Wild Rose Inn will remain one of our homes."

As they entered the inn to celebrate the upcoming

nuptials, Nathaniel and Daisy paused for a moment, staring at one another as though they could hardly believe what all had transpired in so short a time.

"I know this is sudden, Daisy," he said, taking her hand. "But I could not bear for it to be any other way."

"Nor could I," she returned, standing on her toes to kiss him, right there in the doorway, despite who might be walking by. "Nor could I."

EPILOGUE

True to their word, a month later, Daisy and Nathaniel found themselves back at the Wild Rose Inn.

Daisy had been worried throughout their journey to the inn, for she wasn't entirely sure how to approach it. As a guest? As a member of the family who would be put back to work once more? It wasn't as though she could sit there at a table as her sisters cooked for her and served her.

"It will be fine," Nathaniel attempted to reassure her, though Daisy remained concerned.

Fortunately, he proved correct as Marigold had everything prepared. They stayed in one of the guest rooms — the very same one Nathaniel had previously occupied — but lived and dined with the family.

"Tell me," Daisy said eagerly. "What has happened here in the past month?"

"Nothing much," said Marigold, her eyes on her plate as she spoke. "We have new boarders."

"Oh?" Daisy asked, risking a glance over at Nathaniel, wondering if these new guests were soldiers such as him.

"Yes, you are correct," said Marigold, reading into Daisy's unspoken question. "Or, at least, we believe you are. Father has not been entirely forthcoming about the men who have joined us."

Tavners shrugged. "I made a promise to share nothing of their origin — with anyone. And that includes my daughters, who ask more questions than they ever should."

Iris rolled her eyes, causing Daisy to emit a low laugh — until she caught her father's glare and then began coughing to hide her mirth. Iris was many things, but no one else could so accurately respond to some of her father's pronouncements.

"So besides the fact that I'm sure you are not able to say a word about who these men are or what they may be doing here, what are they like? Are they..." she looked over at her husband and winked. "Demanding?"

"Of course not!" her mother exclaimed. "They are lovely."

"Lovely?" repeated Iris. "The one man hardly says a word besides to grunt and emit surly comments on everything around him. One can hardly call him lovely. The other is nice enough, though he has a woman waiting for him at home."

Her cheeks turned pink when she mentioned the last man, which intrigued Daisy. Iris typically had no issue speaking to men of any type. What was different about this one?

"It is good to have them here," her mother finally said. "Especially now that the Johnsons are gone, we need the income."

Daisy nodded, hearing the plea for assistance in her mother's voice, though it was not within her purview to provide it. Through Nathaniel, she knew of her father's gambling lossesf, but not how to help.

"Tell us of your life now, Daisy," Violet said with a sigh. "It must be so lovely. I can hardly imagine it, living as a duchess!"

Daisy smiled at her sister.

"One thing I can tell you is that I am happier than I have ever been," she said, turning her smile to her husband. "For I have married for love, which you must all promise me to do, no matter what may come. But as for my life... I know I am certainly not the most conventional duchess there ever was..."

"But you are perhaps the most intriguing," Nathaniel finished for her. "And by far the most competent."

Daisy's cheeks began to warm, but thankfully Marigold saved her.

"And what of the nobles — the people you were always determined to avoid?" she asked with a hint of a smile at the irony.

"It was wrong of me to cast them all in the same light because of my experiences with a few," Daisy said. "There are many who have been wonderful. I suppose it is like the villagers — some are as friendly as can be while others are only looking out for themselves. I must say that I am met with a good deal of suspicion, as I'm certain most are wondering just how I managed to capture a duke, particularly a young, good looking one at that."

"But," Nathaniel said, taking his wife's hand in his, "None of it matters except for what we have with one another."

Daisy smiled at him, happiness filling her, unlike anything she could ever have before imagined.

LATER THAT NIGHT, Daisy reflected on the mysterious nature of fate as she and Nathaniel lay beside one another in the guest bedroom of the inn where she had been raised.

"Some days I think of what my life would have been — alone, or with Stephen," she shuddered now at the thought of marrying a man like him, "And I can hardly believe how lucky I was — that you looked past the prickly front I provided you to nonetheless take a chance on me."

"And that you overlooked my arrogance. It was the dance," he said with a shrug. "I have always loved to dance, as I told you, and you swept me away."

She laughed. "You cannot mean it."

"Oh, but I do," he said, his brown eyes serious. "I will likely never be able to properly dance with you, my love, but I promise to gently sway with you for the rest of my life."

"I love you, my arrogant Mr. Hawke."

"And I love you, my stubborn Miss Tavners."

Then they proceeded to show one another just exactly how much.

THE END

If you enjoyed A Duke for Daisy, then stay updated on what more is to come! All who sign up for my email list receive "Unmasking a Duke," a regency romance for free — and so much more!

www.prairielilypress.com/ellies-newsletter/

You will also receive links to giveaways, sales, updates, launch information, promos, and the newest recommended reads.

ABOUT THE AUTHOR

Ellie has always loved reading, writing, and history. For many years she has written short stories, non-fiction, and has worked on her true love and passion -- romance novels.

In every era there is the chance for romance, and Ellie enjoys exploring many different time periods, cultures, and geographic locations. No matter when or where, love can always prevail. She has a particular soft spot for the bad boys of history, and loves a strong heroine in her stories.

The lake is Ellie's happy place, and when she's not writing, she is spending time with her son, her Husky/Border Collie cross, and her own dashing duke. She loves reading — of course — as well as running, biking, and summers at the lake.

She also loves corresponding with readers, so be sure to contact her!

www.prairielilypress.com/ellie-st-clair
ellie@prairielilypress.com

facebook.com/elliestclairauthor
twitter.com/ellie_stclair
instagram.com/elliestclairauthor
amazon.com/author/elliestclair
goodreads.com/elliestclair
bookbub.com/authors/elliest.clair
pinterest.com/elliestclair

ALSO BY ELLIE ST. CLAIR

Standalone

Unmasking a Duke

Christmastide with His Countess

Happily Ever After

The Duke She Wished For

Someday Her Duke Will Come

Once Upon a Duke's Dream

He's a Duke, But I Love Him

Loved by the Viscount

Because the Earl Loved Me

Searching Hearts

Duke of Christmas

Quest of Honor

Clue of Affection

Hearts of Trust

Hope of Romance

Promise of Redemption

The Unconventional Ladies

Lady of Mystery

Lady of Fortune

Blooming Brides

A Duke for Daisy

THE DUKE SHE WISHED FOR

HAPPILY EVER AFTER BOOK 1

PREVIEW

Begin the Happily Ever After series with the story of Tabitha and Nicholas...

CHAPTER 1

The creak of the shop's front door opening floated through the heavy curtains that separated Tabitha's workshop from the sales floor. She tensed over the silk ribbon she was attempting to fashion into a flower shape and waited for the sound of her stepsister Frances to greet whoever had just walked into the Blackmore Milliner shop.

She paused, waiting a little bit longer before pushing out a frustrated breath and standing. These velvet ribbon flowers she had learned to fashion were part of the reason Blackmore hats sat atop some of the finest female heads in polite society — she had a knack for creating new ways to adorn the same old bonnet or beaver hat styles so that a woman of a certain class stood out among her peers.

This ability was both a blessing and a curse, it turned out. Her creativity meant Tabitha brought customers through the front door, to the shop she and her father had built after her mother died when she was seven years old. It had brought Tabitha and her father, the baronet Elias Blackmore, closer together in their time of immeasurable grief, and the shop had flourished.

The relationship between father and daughter remained strong, and when she was twelve years of age, he approached her and told her he wanted to marry a baroness from the North Country. The baroness had a daughter about her own age, he'd added. Tabitha had been happy for her father and excited at the prospect of having a sister. She had welcomed her new family with an open heart and open arms.

What a silly little fool she'd been, Tabitha thought with derisive snort as she pushed herself to her feet and through the brocade curtains to greet the newcomer. Lord only knew where Frances had gone off to. Likely shopping with her mother, Ellora.

Upon the untimely death of Sir Elias Blackmore three years after the marriage, Tabitha had been utterly devastated. Lady Blackmore, however, hadn't wasted much time in putting Tabitha in her place. No longer the family's most cherished daughter, Tabitha had been shoved into the workroom and largely ignored, but for her skills as a milliner — they kept just enough of her stepmother's attention on her.

The more she stood up to Ellora, the more her stepmother threatened to throw her out on the street. Knowing it was within Ellora's nature to follow through on her threat, Tabitha did her best to ignore and avoid her stepmother, focusing instead on her work and her ambitions.

It was better, Tabitha supposed, than staying in their townhome all day long worrying about social calls that never came or invitations that would never arrive. The family name had suffered greatly under Lady Blackmore and Miss Frances Denner, her daughter from a previous marriage.

In truth, Tabitha was little more than a servant with no money to speak of, no family to lean on, and no real prospects other than her creations on which to pin her hopes of ever escaping the lot she'd been given after her father died.

In the showroom, Tabitha scanned the floor in search of the new arrival. It took a moment, but her eyes finally landed on a small, older man in a fine suit. He had a slip of paper in his hand, and he approached Tabitha with the air of someone who didn't waste time.

"Good afternoon, Miss," the man began with perfect, practiced speech. "My name is Mr. McEwan. I serve as the steward in the house of Her Grace the Duchess of Stowe. I have a receipt for a series of hats I believe she had ordered, and she is requesting that they be delivered tomorrow afternoon."

Tabitha felt her stomach sink. If this was the order she was thinking of, the one currently on her worktable, there was no way under the stars that the three hats would be ready by tomorrow. She was only one flower (out of seven) into the first bonnet, and it was a slow process to convince the requested velvet ribbon to behave.

"I am sorry, sir," she began, trying to get his eyes off the wilder ostrich-plumed hats next to her and back on her. "That is almost four days before we agreed upon. I'm certain there is no feasible way the work can be done, and done well, by tomorrow."

That got the older man's attention. He huffed, turned a bit pink around the cheeks, and sputtered.

"There is simply no choice, my dear," he said abruptly but not unkindly. "His Grace is arriving home from his trip to France early and therefore the parties his mother has planned for him will be adjusted accordingly. And so, her wardrobe *must* be ready — she said so herself. She is willing to pay handsomely for your ability to expedite the process."

Tabitha drew in a breath at that and considered. She was having such a difficult time scrimping a small savings together to buy herself a seat at the Paris School of Millinery that this "bonus" money might perhaps get her there that much quicker. Assuming, of course, that Ellora didn't catch wind of the extra earnings. She was quick to snatch up all but the barest pennies.

Tabitha closed her eyes for a moment and drew a steadying breath. If she worked through the night and her needle and thread held true, there was a *slight* chance that she could finish in time. She said so to Mr. McEwan, who beamed brightly at her.

"I knew it," he said with a laugh. "I have faith you Miss — er, I apologize, I did not hear your name?"

Tabitha sighed.

"Tabitha Blackmore," she said, noticing how quickly he'd changed the subject on her. "I did not exactly say that I would be able to—"

She was cut off again by Mr. McEwan, who gave her a slight bow and provided directions to the home of the Dowager Duchess of Stowe on the other side of the city.

"I shall see you tomorrow, then, my dear," he said with a quick grin. "Be sure to pack a bag to stay at least one evening, maybe two. I am certain Her Grace's attendants will need proper coaching on how best to pair the hats. You will be paid, of course!"

With that the short man with wisps of white hair on his head that stood up like smoke was gone, disappearing into the streets of Cheapside.

Tabitha leaned back against the counter behind her and blew out a breath, a little overwhelmed at the entire encounter.

On the one hand, she had found a way to increase her

savings and take a step closer to the education her father had wanted for her. On the other, getting through the night in one piece was not guaranteed. She would have to return to the shop after dinner and do so without rousing Lady Blackmore's suspicions, which would not be easy.

Tabitha kicked at a crushed crepe ribbon flower that hadn't been tossed out properly. Another evening down the back drainpipe it was, then.

"Time away from the witch, I suppose," she muttered as she returned to her worktable, a new fire of inspiration lit beneath her.

Dinner was more complicated than usual, thanks to the fact that Ellora, Tabitha's stepmother, was having one of her *moods.* They could be brought on by anything — the weather (too foul or too pleasant), the noisy street they lived on, memories of her life when she was the daughter of an earl and had endless opportunities for money and titles, or even an egg that had too much salt.

Today's mood, however, had more to do with the fact that her daughter Frances had been recently snubbed. Officially, Ellora was considered a member of the *ton* and her daughter's first season the previous year had nearly cost them the roof over their heads. However, Frances was an ill-tempered, sharp-tongued girl who did little to ensure repeat invitations to dances and parties.

"A true-and-true witch," their housekeeper, Alice, called her. Alice was the only servant left on staff besides Katie, the lady's maid Ellora and Frances shared, so it was up to both Alice and Tabitha to make sure that meals were made and rooms were kept clean. Being an indentured servant in her own home was trying enough, but much worse was having to tidy the room that once held every memento of her father's. It was now completely devoid of every memory of him.

It was as though Baronet Elias Blackmore had never existed. No portraits. No personal belongings. Nothing but the small locket he'd given Tabitha when she was nine years old, which she still wore around her neck.

This evening's dinner was a morose affair, and Tabitha sat silently while Ellora ranted and raved about the social snub of her angel, Frances.

Tabitha looked across the table at her stepsister. Frances was very pretty, she'd give her that much. But her mouth was drawn thin and her blue eyes were more steely than pleasant. Frances had brown hair that one could call more dishwater in color than brunette. However, Ellora spent high sums of money on beauty products and bits and bobs for Katie to fashion Frances' hair into something resembling high fashion each day.

Frances was pouting into her soup while her mother railed beside her. When she glanced up and caught Tabitha looking at her, she scowled.

Tabitha quickly looked away, but Frances jumped on the opportunity to take the attention off her.

"I saw a servant go into the shop this afternoon when I was returning from tea with Adela," Frances said to her mother, her flinty eyes on Tabitha, who inwardly groaned.

So much for secrecy.

Ellora paused in her ranting and raised an eyebrow at her.

"Who was it?"

The words were clipped, and her nose was high in the air while she peered along it at Tabitha.

"A servant for the Dowager Duchess of Stowe," Tabitha replied. "He came to inquire about an order the Duchess sent over a week ago."

It wasn't exactly a lie and it helped her corroborate her story because Ellora had already received the money sent over for the original order.

"And was the order ready?"

Tabitha swallowed hard. She wasn't in the clear yet.

"Almost," she said and lowered her eyes to take a sip of the soup as she inwardly seethed.

"Unacceptable," her stepmother ground out between her teeth. "You lazy, no-good hanger-on. It is no wonder your father's ridiculous hat shop is dying off. He had the laziest cow this side of the river working behind the curtains."

She banged a fist on the table, making Frances jump.

"You get up from this table and you finish that order right this instant." Ellora pointed a long bony finger in the direction of the door, ending Tabitha's dinner before she had progressed past the soup. Tabitha's stomach rumbled in protest, and her fists clenched beneath the table as she longed to tell Ellora what she really thought, but Tabitha knew this was a gift. She would nab a roll from Alice later.

"I am going to stop by in the morning to check your ledger and work progress to make certain you are being completely honest with me," Ellora announced. "And woe be to you if I find that you have been neglecting your work and you have a backlog of orders."

In reality, Tabitha was of legal age and the threats should be harmless. But she was also lacking any real money, any job prospects, and had no titles her father could have passed down to her. Running her father's milliner shop was the closest thing she would have to freedom for the near future, and it would be much better for her if she allowed Ellora the illusion of control for the time being, since the dreadful woman had inherited the shop upon her father's death.

Ellora's threat put Tabitha in a bind. She was due at the Duchess' estate first thing in the morning. As it stood, she'd have to have those pieces done, as well as the other orders on her workbench before then. She closed her eyes and blew out a heavy breath.

It was going to be a very long night.

The Duke She Wished For is now available for purchase on Amazon, and is free to read through Kindle Unlimited.

Made in the USA
Lexington, KY
10 June 2019